I0642673

THE
MOSES
QUILT

ENDORSEMENTS

The characters are classic, the plot intriguing, the reading is easy, and the quilt ... mystifying. We'll hold on to the end. When Kathi Macias writes the message, the message will enhance your life!
—**Thelma Wells**, author, speaker, president of A Woman of God Ministries (thelmawells.com)

A love story etched in the fabric of time. A man and woman from opposite worlds brought close by love, an heirloom quilt, and two great women of faith. Just as the quilt transcended the ages, can their love survive?
—**Bonnie Calhoun**, publisher of *Christian Fiction Online Magazine* and author of *Cooking the Books*

What an amazing woman of faith and an astounding read about the personal sacrifices made to help others be free! And what a strong and personal call, not only to Edward and Mazie but to all of us to walk out our faith and courage in our everyday lives. After reading this book, you'll never look at quilts, courage, or Harriet Tubman the same way
—**Nora St. Laurent**, CEO, Book Club Network (bookfun.org)

*The Moses Quilt i*s a contemporary story that focuses on two people who must find a way to bridge the racial and generational divide that stands between them. Author Kathi Macias weaves a charming story that both entertains and challenges readers to look at their own prejudices.

—**Karen O'Connor,** best-selling author, *The Beauty of Aging* and *When God Answers Your Prayers*

An intricate patchwork of history, love lost, and hope found, *The Moses Quilt* spans generations and secrets to blanket all in God's grace. Delightful!

—**Patti Lacy**, author of *Reclaiming Lily* and *What the Bayou Saw*

THE
MOSES
QUILT

KATHI MACIAS

A Christian Company
ElkLakePublishingInc.com

COPYRIGHT NOTICE

The Moses Quilt

Second edition. Copyright © 2024 by Kathi Macias. The information contained in this book is the intellectual property of Kathi Macias and is governed by United States and International copyright laws. All rights reserved. No part of this publication, either text or image, may be used for any purpose other than personal use. Therefore, reproduction, modification, storage in a retrieval system, or retransmission, in any form or by any means, electronic, mechanical, or otherwise, for reasons other than personal use, except for brief quotations for reviews or articles and promotions, is strictly prohibited without prior written permission by the publisher.

This is a work of fiction. Names, characters, businesses, places, events, locales, and incidents are either the products of the author's imagination or used in a fictitious manner. Any resemblance to actual persons, living or dead, or actual events is purely coincidental.

Scriptures are taken from the NEW KING JAMES VERSION (NKJV): Scripture taken from the NEW KING JAMES VERSION®. Copyright© 1982 by Thomas Nelson, Inc. Used by permission. All rights reserved.

Cover and Interior Design: Kelly Artieri, Deb Haggerty
Editor(s): Judy Hagey, Cristel Phelps, Deb Haggerty

PUBLISHED BY: Elk Lake Publishing, Inc., 35 Dogwood Drive, Plymouth, MA 02360, 2024

Library Cataloging Data
Names: Macias, Kathi, (Kathi Macias)
The Moses Quilt / Kathi Macias
245 p. 23cm × 15cm (9in × 6 in.)
ISBN-13: 9798891341715 (paperback) | 9798891341722 (trade paperback) | 9798891341739 (e-book)
Key Words: Harriett Tubman; biracial relationships; quilt fans; intergenerational relationships; unresolved personal conflicts; inherited prejudice; interwoven historical/contemporary
Library of Congress Control Number: 2024934010 Fiction

DEDICATION

To my dear husband, whose love and support encourages me to press on when I'm weary.

And to all the courageous and forgiving hearts that have crossed the spans of time and bridged the chasms of Black and White, good and evil, fear and hatred—thank you. You honor the memory of such great heroes as Harriet Tubman, Martin Luther King Jr., and—most of all—the Lord Jesus Christ himself.

PROLOGUE

Edward's eyes captivated her as they always did. Their warm, chocolate pools bid her to abandon herself to their delicious charm. And oh, how she wanted to do so! But something—always, there was a nameless something—held her back, restraining her from yielding to the joy she so longed to experience.

"I can't," she whispered. "I just can't. Not yet. Soon, I promise, but ..."

The light in his gaze flickered, and she knew she'd hurt him ... again. She hadn't wanted to, had even told herself that this time, today, she would give him her answer. But she just wasn't ready.

Her heart squeezed. Would she ever be? Could she ever get past the unnamed fear that haunted her life, threatening to squeeze the air from her lungs. What was it that frightened her to the point she couldn't move forward, couldn't give a good man a simple answer—particularly when that man made her head swim with longing?

"Soon," he repeated, his husky voice devoid of bitterness or sarcasm. "How many times have you promised, Mazie? How many?"

Tears bit her eyes, and she shook her head. "Too many," she said. "Far too many. And I'm truly sorry, but I ..."

Resignation washed over his face as he loosened his embrace and took a small step back, his eyes never breaking from hers. "I wish I could say I understand, but I don't." His smile was wistful as he used a finger to brush back a stray wisp of dark hair from her face. "But I will honor your feelings. I know I need to stop pushing, and I will, though it won't be easy. I love you, Mazie. You know that."

Her breath caught, and she nodded. If she knew anything in this world, it was that Edward Clayton loved her, and that he was an honorable man. She was a fool for putting him off like this, but how could she give him an answer when she was so unsure about ... everything?

"Thank you," she whispered. "For loving me and for giving me more time."

The pain skittered through his eyes again, outlined by the setting sun that filtered through the trees behind him. He leaned down and planted a soft kiss on her forehead. "Let me know when you're ready," he said. Then he turned and walked toward his car parked in the driveway, leaving Mazie standing alone on the porch with the first of many hot tears spilling over onto her cheeks.

As she watched him drive away, she shoved down the nagging questions that had haunted her since she first fell in love with Edward. *Am I ready to enter into a permanent relationship with a man of another race? Will my Southern born-and-bred great-grandmother really accept him and his family—100 percent?* Mimi had assured Mazie more than once that she adored Edward, but was she truly ready for her own flesh and blood to marry an African American man, no matter how much the beloved elderly woman claimed to care for him? *But there's more, I know there is—not with*

Mimi so much but with me. What is the fear that's holding me back, and how do I get past it so I can follow my heart and say yes to the man I love?

With a heavy sigh, Mazie turned from the window and headed for the kitchen.

CHAPTER ONE

Mazie Hartford hadn't set foot in Prattville, Alabama, since she was eight years old—nearly sixteen years ago—but she would never forget the summer she spent there, visiting her great-grandmother. Even the locals said it was the hottest July and August any of them could remember, and Mazie was certain that was true. Anything hotter would have killed them all, and the young girl imagined that even if she'd had some serious unforgiven sins on her account and she'd ended up in hell, it couldn't have been any worse than the attic bedroom she'd been assigned when she first arrived.

She sat now on the wide front porch of her mother's home, overlooking the fertile valley less than a thirty-minute drive from San Francisco. Though slightly inland from the City by the Bay, Mazie's little hometown of Langsdale benefited from the cool breezes and nearly ever-present fog so common to the Bay Area. Even now, as the thin rays of the early morning sun fought to break through the gray overcast of early summer, she remembered the shock of walking out of the Selma, Alabama, airport and feeling as if she'd been slapped in the face with a giant hot towel. Within seconds, her dark curls had turned to damp ringlets frizzing around her face as great drops of perspiration trickled down her back. And yet her great-grandmother had hobbled along beside her on her cane, chatting excitedly as they made their way with Mazie's aunt and uncle toward their car—as if there were nothing unusual about the broiling temperature that took the child's breath away.

Is it always like this? Mazie had wondered. *Is it going to be this hot the whole time I'm here? Will it at least cool down at night?*

She soon learned that it didn't—not much, anyway. And when first they'd taken her home from the airport and escorted her to the room in the attic, which was twice as hot as outside, Mazie had considered turning around and making a mad dash back to the plane. Surely she would die up here in this closed, airless room. Didn't they see it? Her aunt had explained the air conditioner just didn't quite make it up that far, but it was the only spare room they had, and she was sure Mazie would adapt. Mazie was sure she wouldn't and soon enlisted her great-grandmother's help to lobby for a bed for her out on the screened-in porch where an occasional puff of breeze brought a wisp of relief. And so the eight-year-old had survived what was otherwise a very pleasant summer with her mother's sister and brother-in-law, and of course, the indomitable great-grandma Mazie, affectionately known as Mimi, after whom the young girl was named.

"Mazie girl, you out there?"

The familiar voice, somehow melodic despite sounding like the grating of a pile of rusty tin cans, brought a smile to the girl's lips. How she had missed her great-grandmother after returning home from her visit to the deep, hot South! She had never dreamed the feisty old woman would one day live in California with her and her mother, but here she was—as she had been for the last five years since Mazie's aunt and uncle had relocated to Costa Rica.

"Costa Rica," the family matriarch had bemoaned, repeating her complaint only slightly less often now than when she'd first come to live with them. "Who lives in Costa Rica? Who even goes there? Why, when I was a girl I never even heard of the place."

Mazie knew it had broken her great-grandmother's heart to leave her home behind and move across the country to a place called California where she'd never been, but move she had. The only other alternative had been a rest home, and Mazie's mother wouldn't hear of it. So now there were the three of them—daughter, mother, and great-grandmother—living under one roof. And though Mazie knew the dear old woman still missed Alabama, she also suspected the nonagenarian had come to enjoy her new residence.

"Yes, Mimi," she called out. "I'm out here sitting on the porch, having my morning tea."

"Humph." The sound drifted through the screen door, and Mazie could picture the old woman's lined face, her lips drawn together in disapproval. "You're going to catch your death out there one of these days," she grumbled. "How many times have I warned you about going out there before the sun burns through those clouds? And you know that wind's blowing in from the ocean. You're going to catch your death, I'm telling you. Leastwise back home, a person could stay warm most of the time."

Still smiling, Mazie stood, leaving her nearly empty tea mug on the tiny table near her rocking chair before walking to the door. "All right, Mimi. I'm coming inside."

She opened the door and spotted the shriveled-up woman, whom she loved so dearly, hunched over in her wheelchair where Mazie's mother had parked her near the front window beside the door. "Have you had your breakfast yet?" Mazie asked.

The old woman wrinkled her forehead, and Mazie realized she would be raising her eyebrows if she still had any. "You know your mama had to go to work early this morning, so how would I have any breakfast? Can't hardly fix anything myself, stuck in this wheelchair, you know."

"I know, Mimi," Mazie said, bending down to kiss her forehead. Though the woman's skin was nearly paper thin, it was still soft, and Mazie marveled. She imagined she would always think her great-grandmother was the most beautiful woman she'd ever known. "Come on," she said, grabbing the handles of the wheelchair and pushing toward the kitchen. "Let's see what we can find to eat. I may not be much of a cook, but I think I can manage a couple bowls of oatmeal and some toast."

"Humph."

Mazie grinned. She knew her great-grandma was thinking oatmeal and toast didn't suffice as an adequate breakfast, but Mazie also knew she'd do her best to eat it once it was set in front of her—because, after all, that was the way she was brought up.

They'd made it through breakfast and were sipping a final cup of tea when Mazie's cell phone jingled. She ignored her great-grandmother's look of disapproval and dug the phone out of her pocket, peeking at the caller ID. Her heart did a quick sidestep when she saw Edward's name, and she flipped it open.

"Hello?"

"Good morning," came the voice that flowed over her heart like warm honey. "Just thought I'd check in and see how everything's going for you today."

She knew he was restraining himself from talking about the things that mattered most to him, and that knowledge only increased her admiration for him. "I ... we're fine," she answered, glancing briefly at the old woman who sat across from her, eyes squinted and lips puckered. "I'm just sitting here at the table with Mimi, finishing our breakfast."

"I thought that's what you might be doing about now," Edward said. "Give her my love, will you?"

"Edward sends his love," she said, directing her words across the table."

Mimi nodded, a hint of a smile playing on her lips. "And mine to him," she said.

Mazie knew her great-grandmother dearly loved Edward, as did Mazie's mother, and she imagined both women wondered why she dragged her feet when it came to responding to his marriage proposal. She also knew there was no apparent reason for her indecision, other than a fear she couldn't identify, something far beyond any concerns about an interracial marriage that was, after all, quite common today. And Mazie had to admit, the timing couldn't be better. Edward was safely ensconced in his father's law firm, ready to take on a wife and family, while she had just graduated college with a degree firmly tucked in her pocket and a teaching job ready to start in the fall. She'd put Edward off the last couple of years because of her studies, but what was her excuse now? She had none.

"Mimi sends her love to you too," she said, envisioning the smile her words would bring to Edward's face.

"So what are you two going to do the rest of the day?"

She shrugged, though she knew he couldn't see her. "I'm not sure. It looks like the sun is going to burn through the fog soon, so if it's warm enough, I'll take Mimi for a walk and maybe even out to lunch later."

Mazie saw her great-grandma's invisible eyebrows rise again, and she smiled. "What about you?" she asked Edward.

He sighed. "I have a major workload today. I'd love to break away and meet the two of you for lunch, but I just don't see that happening."

The thought flitted through her mind that she should invite him for dinner that evening, but she hesitated. Would they get back into their usual discussion about marriage? Would he pressure her again for an answer? But he'd promised the night before he wouldn't, and he was a man of his word.

"What about this evening?" she asked, deciding to trust his promise to give her more time. "Would you like to stop by for dinner? I'll be home all afternoon anyway, so maybe I'll throw something together for all of us. I'm sure Mom would appreciate coming home to a hot meal."

"Humph."

Mazie didn't look up at the sound of the old woman's grunt of disapproval. She knew her great-grandmother didn't think much of her cooking abilities—or lack thereof—but she also knew they would all have a nice visit together if Edward came over after work.

"I'd like that," Edward said, the smile evident in his voice. "I might not be able to make it until close to seven, though. Is that too late?"

"That'll be fine. We'll look forward to it."

"So will I." He paused, and when she didn't say anything more, he added, "See you then," and clicked off.

Mazie closed her phone and stuck it back in her pocket before returning her attention to her great-grandmother, who studied her with unveiled curiosity. Mazie smiled and took one last sip of lukewarm tea before standing to clear the table.

The "original Mazie," as she liked to think of herself, sat in the meager shaft of sunlight that shone through the window by the front door and warmed her only slightly. What in the world were people thinking when they praised this dismal area of the world, even writing songs to commemorate its charm? So far as Mimi was concerned, there was nothing charming about it.

She darted her eyes toward the hallway, wondering how much longer it would be before her great-granddaughter reappeared to take her on their so-called outing. She shivered at the thought of going out in the cool, damp air, but it was better than spending the entire day cooped up inside the house, watching game shows and soap operas.

How had her life come to this? Born and raised in the nice, warm South, where people knew how to cook food that stuck to your ribs and spoke slowly enough that you could understand what they said, she now lived out her final days where the color gray epitomized everything from the weather to the cuisine.

"Salad is good for you, Mimi," Mazie repeated nearly every time they went out to eat. "And maybe a little piece of broiled fish or chicken on the side."

Humph. Broiled indeed. What was wrong with frying chicken or fish and giving it a little flavor? And oh, what she wouldn't give to trade in her morning bowl of oatmeal for some bacon and grits! If she could just get up out of her wheelchair, she'd show these two younger women she lived with how cooking was supposed to be done.

She sighed. At ninety-three, that was just not going to happen, and she might as well accept it. Her cooking days—

and apparently her days of enjoying food, period—were behind her now. If she didn't know for certain she'd step into the presence of her Savior the minute she breathed her last here on earth, she didn't think she'd make it through another day.

The sound of a door opening down the hallway caught her attention, though it was muffled even through her hearing aids. She lifted her head and peered in the direction of Mazie's room, and sure enough, here she came. The girl was already wearing a light jacket—certainly not enough to ward off the cold Bay Area weather in Mimi's opinion—so that meant they were ready to go.

"All set?" Mazie asked as she joined her great-grandmother by the door.

"Been ready since breakfast," Mimi said. "Just waiting on you."

Mazie smiled, and Mimi thought as she so often did what a lovely young woman Mazie had become. Mimi just hoped the girl would hurry up and marry that good-looking Edward Clayton before he lost interest and found someone else, leaving Mazie to become an old maid. Was Mazie dragging her feet because Edward was Black? Mimi had to admit there were certain family members in the South who would be upset over that—scandalized even—but she prided herself on not being one of them.

"I'll get your jacket," Mazie said, opening the door to the closet in the entryway.

"Get the warm one," Mimi ordered. "And a scarf for my neck. I don't want to catch my death out there in the cold."

Mazie was still smiling when she turned back, jacket in hand. "Okay, Mimi. Let's get this on first, and then, I'll get your warm scarf."

Mimi ignored the stiffness in her shoulders as she lifted first one arm and then the other, struggling to get them into the sleeves as Mazie helped. "I suppose that's all you're going to wear," Mimi commented, glancing up at her great-granddaughter's unzipped windbreaker.

"That's it, Mimi. I'll be fine."

"Humph."

She watched Mazie disappear down the hall again and then return a moment later with the knit scarf. Mimi knew she'd still be cold, but she supposed she would have to make do. After all, this wasn't Alabama, and nothing was going to change here anytime soon, leastwise not until she finally made it home to heaven.

CHAPTER TWO

"Mazie? Mimi? Anybody home?"

Lilly stood in the open doorway and listened to the distant sound of voices—not those of her daughter or grandmother, so no doubt the TV playing in Mimi's room. Lilly knew her grandmother didn't really care about the programs that were on most of the time, but she said the sound and flickering images kept her company.

Lilly sighed at the thought. Would she one day be like her grandmother—with her life behind her and nothing or no one to keep her company but mindless television programs?

Only if I live that long. And that's doubtful.

She closed the door behind her and turned toward the kitchen, her nostrils twitching at the first hints of chicken and garlic. Lilly smiled. Mazie might not be the best cook in the world—or even in their three-woman household for that matter—but anything would be welcome tonight. Lilly's feet hurt from standing on them all day. If she'd had to do one more haircut or perm before closing up shop and heading home that evening, she doubted she would have made it. As it was, her last appointment of the day had canceled, and she was more than happy to flip the Open sign to Closed and make a beeline for her car.

"Something smells delicious," she called as she stepped into the kitchen and caught sight of her daughter standing at the sink.

Mazie turned and grinned. "You're being kind," she said. "You know my cooking doesn't qualify as delicious, but it'll fill us up."

Lilly laughed. "Anything I don't have to come home and cook is delicious to me." She flopped down in a chair at the table and kicked off her shoes. "So what's the occasion? Is Edward coming over?"

She noticed her daughter's cheeks flushed as she nodded. "I'd ask how you knew, but I guess that's obvious, isn't it?"

"After all this time? I would say so, yes." Lilly smiled. "I know you don't like me to pry, but when in the world are you two finally going to make your relationship permanent? The guy is crazy about you, you know."

"I do know. And we're talking about it." Mazie also knew her mom would be the last person in their family or neighborhood to be concerned about their racial issue.

Lilly shook her head. "What's to talk about? Seriously, Mazie, it's not like you two don't know each other by now. You're perfect together."

Mazie tilted her head and opened her mouth as if she were about to say something but instead turned back to the sink and turned on the water to rinse a head of lettuce. "Like I said, we're talking about it, Mom. Let's just leave it at that, shall we?"

Lilly knew when she'd been dismissed. She sighed. Fine. She'd leave it alone—for now. But only because she knew that once her daughter had made up her mind, there was simply no changing it until she was good and ready. Meanwhile, Lilly might as well slip down the hall and check on her grandmother. She was certain she'd have no trouble tearing her away from her program—unless, of course, one of her favorite TV preachers happened to be on. Then Lilly and everyone else would just have to wait.

Edward thought he'd never get used to being so warmly welcomed by a Southern belle—and one in her nineties at that. Mimi, as she insisted he call her, was everything he somehow envisioned as being a bigot or even a racist. And yet, she was the furthest thing from it. Cantankerous as she might be, she had evidently allowed herself to examine and judge him with a fair and open mind, and they had soon become fast friends. If anything, he knew she lobbied on his behalf when it came to the reticent young woman who was her namesake. Mazie's mother also championed his cause of wanting to marry the younger Mazie—it was only Mazie herself who seemed unable to make the commitment.

He mounted the porch in front of their home and rang the doorbell, his mouth already watering at the aromas drifting through the screen door. Thankfully, he'd finished up at work a bit sooner than expected and hadn't kept everyone waiting too long.

Mazie answered the door, her cheeks flushed and her scooped-up hair trailing dark tendrils around her face. Edward grinned. She'd been cooking, and he knew what that meant. What the dinner lacked in quality would be made up for in quantity, and right now, as hungry as he was, that was just fine with him.

"Hey," he said, stepping inside as she opened the screen door. He kissed her warm cheek and whispered, "Is that *eau de garlic* I smell?"

"Very funny," she teased, turning back toward the kitchen as he followed close behind. "I'll have you know I've been working in this hot kitchen all afternoon, so you'd better show some respect and appreciation for all my trouble, Edward Clayton."

Edward caught sight of Mimi sitting in her wheelchair by the table and winked. "Yes, ma'am," he crooned. "I will certainly do that."

The old woman returned his wink and smiled as he headed toward her and bent down to give her a hug and kiss.

"Don't let her buffalo you," Mimi said. "She may have been in the kitchen for the past couple of hours, but it's not that much work to make a casserole and a salad. And besides, it's not hot here at all. Why, I've nearly forgotten what hot feels like."

She laughed then, and Edward joined her. "I guess you left hot behind in Alabama, didn't you?"

Mimi nodded, the white bun on top of her head bobbing with her. "I surely did," she agreed. "And oh, what I wouldn't give to feel it just one more time before I die."

"Oh now, Mimi," Lilly said, interrupting them as she popped into the kitchen, "it's not that bad. We keep this house nice and warm for you, you know that. And besides, the sun's been out most of the day."

"Humph. You call that puny sunshine warm? Why, I can remember winter nights back in Prattville that were warmer than that."

As he basked in the warm family banter, Edward moved on to greet the woman he hoped would soon be his mother-in-law with a hug. He loved being around this trio of women and felt so at home here. Now if he could just convince the youngest of the three she should agree to become his wife.

Stepping up behind her, he leaned in close and said, "What can I do to help? Set the table? Slice the tomatoes?"

She glanced up at him, the smile in her dark eyes more convincing than the one on her lips. "You just go sit down and relax. You've been working all day. I'll have this dinner on the table in a jiffy."

"Are you sure?"

"Go on," she insisted. "Really. It's all under control."

Edward nodded and kissed her cheek again before turning to join the other women at the table. He knew better than to try to arm wrestle Mazie into anything—whether it was helping with dinner or getting married. So, he might as well just sit this one out until she was ready.

"You look tired, Mimi."

"I am. But it was a nice evening, wasn't it?"

Mazie smiled and nodded. She'd enjoyed the entire event, particularly since Edward hadn't brought up marriage even once. Of course, that may have been because they were never alone, but whatever the reason, Mazie appreciated it. "It was," she agreed. "Even my dinner turned out okay, don't you think?"

"It was very nice, child." The old woman yawned as Mazie helped her transfer from her wheelchair to her bed.

"Here, Mimi," she said, "I'll help you get your nightgown on."

Mazie knew it was a struggle for the elderly lady to get in and out of her clothes each morning and evening, and Mazie did her best to make it as easy on her as possible.

Now that summer had arrived, and she was between school and starting work in the fall, the primary task of caring for her great-grandmother had fallen to her—since her own mother worked full-time at the beauty shop she'd owned for years and appreciated any help Mazie could give her. The very thought of all her mother had sacrificed to put her through school caused Mazie's heart to swell with gratitude, particularly since she knew her father hadn't lived long enough to provide much for his family after he was gone. Mazie scarcely remembered him, except through photographs in family albums and a few snapshots in her mind. She knew he'd been a good and decent man— everyone said so—but beyond that, it was all a bit hazy, particularly since his immediate family had never had much contact with them. Mazie's childhood memories consisted mostly of herself and her mother—with the special summer she'd spent in Prattville a highlighted interlude.

She smiled as she helped her great-grandmother tug the gown over her head and past her stiff shoulders. In moments, the two of them had maneuvered her into bed and propped her up on the pillows.

"I'm exhausted," Mimi wheezed, her eyes fluttering. "That just wore me out."

Mazie sat down on the side of the bed and took her hand. "I know it did," she said, bending down to kiss Mimi's forehead. "Maybe you'll sleep well tonight."

The old woman opened her eyes. "Maybe," she sighed. "Though it doesn't seem to matter how tired I am when I go to bed. The minute I close my eyes and tell myself to go to sleep, I'm wide awake. I get more sleep dozing in my chair during the day than I do here at night."

"Let's hope tonight's different," Mazie said, swallowing a smile at the thought of how often she'd peeked in on Mimi during the night and found her sound asleep, though the dear old woman would complain the next morning she hadn't slept a wink.

Mimi nodded, and Mazie stood up to leave the room. She'd just about reached the door when her great-grandmother's voice stopped her.

"Mazie girl," she said, still breathing a bit harder than usual, "stay a minute, will you?"

Mazie lifted her eyebrows and turned back. "Sure. I'm in no hurry."

She started back toward the bed, but once again the old woman interrupted her progress. "Wait. Before you sit down here, I want you to get something for me."

"What do you need, Mimi? Some water? Another blanket?"

"Both would be nice, child, but that's not what I had in mind." She lifted a hand and pointed to the cedar chest in the corner. "Open that. I want to show you something."

Mazie felt her eyes widen. Mimi was going to let her see something in her cedar chest? From the time Mazie had visited her great-grandmother in Alabama, she'd been told never to open that chest without permission—and Mimi had never given it. Mazie had no idea what was inside, but she'd always wondered. Was she truly about to find out?

"Open it carefully," the old woman instructed. "What I want you to see is right on top, carefully folded and wrapped in paper. Get it out and bring it here to me."

Obediently Mazie opened the chest, not surprised at the squeak that greeted her as she disturbed the ancient hinges. Sure enough, there on top lay what appeared to be a colorful patchwork quilt, folded and preserved in a layer of white paper. Almost reverently, Mazie lifted it from the chest and walked it over to her great-grandmother's bed.

"Is this it?" Mazie asked.

The wrinkled woman smiled and nodded, and Mazie detected a hint of tears in her faded, rheumy eyes. Obviously the quilt had special meaning to her great-grandmother. Mazie's heart quickened to think she might be about to learn that meaning—but why? She knew her great-grandmother didn't do things capriciously. There was always a reason, not to mention strategic timing.

As Mazie sat down on the edge of the bed, carefully laying the folded quilt between herself and Mimi, she somehow sensed she was about to embark on an adventure that could change the entire course of her life.

CHAPTER THREE

"You may find this hard to believe," Mimi explained as Mazie carefully unwrapped the seemingly ancient but perfectly preserved quilt, "but I've been thinking a lot about this quilt lately, knowing my time is getting close, and I think it's time I passed it on to you."

Mazie gasped and jerked her gaze from the quilt to Mimi's face. Did the old woman mean what she was saying? Was she truly going to pass on one of her most prized possessions, so cherished that Mazie had never even seen it before this night?

"Why ... would you do that?" she whispered, clearing her throat and then repeating the question more loudly so her great-grandmother could hear.

"Because it's time," she said. "If I wait much longer, I'll be dead, and the story behind this quilt would be lost. And that, dear child, would be a much greater tragedy than my passing from this world." The old woman smiled. "And I do believe the telling of the quilt's story just might answer some questions of your own right about now—which is why I'm passing it on to you instead of your mother."

Mazie lifted her eyebrows. What questions could a very old quilt possibly answer for her? The only things she wrestled with in her heart were whether to marry Edward—and why she hesitated in the first place. Mazie couldn't imagine how a quilt could address such issues, no matter what the story behind it.

"I know what you're thinking," Mimi said. "But you just need to be patient and listen, like you did when you were a little girl, and we sat out on the screened-in porch together in Alabama. You remember those days?"

Mazie nodded. How could she ever forget? It was the first time she'd ever been away from home without her mother, the first time she'd been in a state other than California, and the first time she'd met the Southern portion of their family. As happy as she'd been to return to the cool temperatures of the Bay Area, she knew she'd left a part of her heart back in Alabama. Was she now about to have that portion of her heart restored through her great-grandmother's story about a quilt?

"This here," Mimi said, lifting a corner of the precious cloth, "is my Moses quilt." She smiled. "You know why it's called that?"

Mazie shook her head. "I have no idea." She returned her great-grandmother's smile. "But I'm hoping you're about to tell me."

"I surely am." The old woman smiled again. "But the story's going to take a lot longer than one night. We'll start it now and work on it one patch at a time. We'll begin with one of my favorite patches, right here in the middle."

She used her gnarled finger to point to a spot near the center of the quilt. Mazie leaned closer and squinted at the brown shape against a blue background. "It ... looks like a baby's cradle," she said.

Mimi nodded. "Exactly. This patch represents the first five years in the life of a woman who came to be known as the Moses of her people. Do you know who I mean?"

Mazie frowned. She'd heard the term somewhere ... Ah, of course! She nodded. "Harriet Tubman. The woman who escaped slavery and then went back and led others out too. So this quilt was named for her?"

"Named for her because it was made to represent her life—and an amazing life it was. Do you know she made nineteen trips back into the South, where some say there was a huge price on her head—dead or alive—and she brought out some three hundred slaves. Never lost a one, including most of her family members." She shook her head. "By rights, she should've been caught or killed, but God had His hand on that brave woman, and nothing was going to stop her from rescuing as many souls as she could."

"So this square here," Mazie asked, "represents her life as a little girl?"

"It does," Mimi said. "But don't go thinking that means she had a nice little cradle like that and a pleasant childhood, because that poor child had anything but. Let me tell you just a little bit about what it was like for this Moses of her people when she was just a tiny girl."

Mazie moved back to the chair, realizing her great-grandmother was on a roll now, so she might as well make herself comfortable while she tried to figure out how a story about the life of Harriet Tubman could possibly answer the questions that stirred in the depth of her own soul.

"Harriet Tubman wasn't her name when she was born on the eastern shore of Maryland," Mimi explained. "Her parents were Ben and Harriet Ross, and they named her Araminta or Minty, but she took her mama's name when she got a little older. Most believe Harriet was born in 1820, but others have reported it as a few years earlier or later. Accurate records were hard to come by in those days, especially for slaves, and even the books that have been written about Harriet over the years are based on educated guesses and oral history. But one thing we know for sure—Araminta Ross, or Harriet Tubman, was an exceptional woman with uncompromising faith. And it was that faith that drove her to live so nobly and courageously."

Mazie touched the square that showed the tiny cradle. "So she must have been very poor as a child."

Mimi laughed. "Harriet Tubman was poor her whole life. Everything she ever got she gave away or sold to help someone else. She lived poor, and she died poor, but she was richer than you or I can ever imagine."

"Do you know what her earliest years were like?"

"She no doubt grew up in a ramshackle slave shack, maybe a hundred yards or so from the big house, where their owners, the Brodas family, lived. The shacks had dirt floors and no windows, and the families who lived there didn't have much food. Most lived on salted fish or pork, corn meal mush, and potatoes—and they were glad to have it, believe me. And since Harriet had five brothers and six sisters, that family had to make those food rations last."

Mazie felt her eyes widen. As an only child, she'd spent a lot of her time dreaming about what it would be like to have siblings and feeling more than slightly cheated that she didn't. But to be one of a dozen children, born into such poverty with little or no hope of any improvement? It was almost more than she could imagine.

"And don't think those early years of Harriet's life were spent playing with her brothers and sisters and enjoying a carefree life," Mimi cautioned. "Like all the other youngsters on the Brodas Plantation, Harriet was looked after by a slave whose job it was to keep the little ones out of mischief long enough to survive the first five years or so of their pitiful existence."

"And then?"

"And then, they were put to work, either in the master's house or out in the fields. There was no time for play, no chance for an education, and no fairness in the way they were treated. Harriet's life was hard and cruel from the very beginning, though she was born into a loving family who shared her great faith in a good God and an ultimate deliverance, even if they had to wait until they died to experience it."

Tears bit Mazie's eyes as she considered the young child being forced into such a cruel life. How did Harriet manage to grasp and maintain a strong faith with so much evil around her? Then again, without it, how could she possibly have survived?

Before she could ask, Mimi's eyes fluttered shut, and she whispered, "That's all for tonight, child. I'm so very tired now. Tomorrow night, I will tell you more about the Moses quilt. For now, I must try to sleep."

Mazie kissed her great-grandmother's forehead once again, laid the quilt on the chair where she'd been sitting, and tiptoed from the room, turning out the light before closing the door behind her.

Mazie had agreed to meet Edward for lunch the next day, so long as Mimi was doing well and able to stay on her own for a couple of hours. Though the old woman had complained about the cold and damp most of the morning, not to mention she claimed not to have slept well during the night, she shooed Mazie out of the house when she learned about the lunch date.

"I'll be just fine here by myself," she insisted. "I've had my breakfast, and now I'm ready for a little nap before my afternoon shows start. Maybe you could bring me a tuna fish sandwich when you come back, though. That would be nice."

Mazie had promised to do so, checked in on Mimi one last time, and headed out the door. The drive to Clayton and Clayton Law Offices took less than fifteen minutes, and Mazie maneuvered it without paying much attention to the familiar scenery. Though the streets and roads in and around Langsdale meandered through rolling hills, they weren't nearly as steep as in the nearby city of San Francisco, and the landscape was much more rural. Even when she reached the downtown area where the law firm was located, the setting seemed more country than city, and for that, Mazie was grateful. Though she had many fond memories of visiting various sites within San Francisco proper, she had no desire to live or work in such a thriving metropolis—especially now that it was nearly overrun with homeless, and many businesses had closed or moved away.

She squeezed her five-year-old Toyota Camry into a diagonal space in front of the offices and hopped out, snagging her purse before she closed the door. The sun had finally managed to break through the fog, and she smiled at its welcome warmth, thinking how Mimi would still insist it was cold.

Letting herself in the front door, she smiled in welcome as Tracy, the receptionist and Edward's younger sister, looked up.

"Hey," Tracy said, her face lighting up as she rose from her seat. "I heard you were coming." She came around to the front of her desk and pulled Mazie into a hug. "Edward told me as soon as he came in this morning."

Mazie pulled back and smiled. "He asked me last night, before he left our place. I'm glad it worked out."

"Me too." Tracy was still smiling. "So where are you two going?"

"I'm not sure." Mazie shrugged. "We didn't get that far in our discussion. Mom had to work today, so I had to make sure Mimi was all right before I made any definite plans."

Tracy nodded. "I love that you take such good care of your great-grandma. It says a lot about you."

Mazie's cheeks warmed. "Not really. She's family, after all. Anyone would do it."

"Not necessarily. I've known a lot of elderly people who just wish their family members would call them or come by once in a while, let alone take care of them." She shook her head. "No. You and your mom are very special to take care of that precious Mimi of yours." She grinned. "So I assume, since you're here, she must be doing well."

"As well as can be expected for ninety-three, I suppose. I left her napping and anticipating her afternoon TV shows, but she also asked me to bring her a tuna sandwich when I come back."

Tracy chuckled. "Sounds like Mimi. Well, hold on a minute, and I'll let Edward know you're here. Or you can just take a chance and go on in if you'd like. You're the one exception to his 'no interruptions' rule."

Mazie smiled. "No, you go ahead and buzz him. I'll wait."

Tracy walked back to her side of the desk, but before she could press the buzzer on the phone, one of the two doors behind her opened, and Edward appeared.

"I thought I heard voices out here," he said, his smile spreading across his handsome face. "Specific voices, actually." He walked toward Mazie, his arms outstretched, stopping just inches in front of her. "I'm glad you made it."

"So am I." She smiled up at him, her heart skipping a beat as it did each time she saw him. When he placed a quick peck on her lips, she asked herself for perhaps the thousandth time what she was waiting for, why she didn't just accept his proposal and get on with it. The man was as close to perfect as anyone could ever be, and she'd be a fool to let him go.

"All right, you two lovebirds," Tracy interrupted. "This is a place of business, you know."

Edward and Mazie smiled at one another but didn't break eye contact. "Sounds like my little sis thinks we should take this somewhere else," Edward said. "What do you think? Anywhere in particular you'd like to go eat?"

"Surprise me," Mazie said.

Edward nodded. "All right. You asked for it. A surprise it is."

With that, he turned to Tracy and said, "I'll be back in an hour or so—probably more like 'or so.' I'll have my cell if you need me in the meantime." Then he took Mazie's elbow and propelled her out the front door, his touch sending a shiver down the young woman's spine that even the noonday sun couldn't dispel.

"What in the world made you think of this place?"

Edward smiled, enjoying the delight he saw shining on Mazie's face. The sparkle in her dark eyes told him he'd made the right choice.

He shrugged. "You said I should surprise you, so ... surprise!"

Mazie laughed, throwing her arms out and spinning in a circle, sending Edward's heart into double time as she tilted her face upward toward the sky. Would she ever get past the fears and reservations that held her back from making a commitment to him? Though she swore it wasn't their obvious differences that fueled those fears, Edward couldn't imagine what else it could be. If she'd just admit to it, he was sure they could work it out.

"I love picnics," Mazie exclaimed, stopping her twirling to gaze up into his eyes. "And this is the perfect place for one."

Edward had to agree. The small clearing overlooked the valley below and enjoyed the full impact of the sun without being uncomfortably warm, since the sea breezes reached them even at this slightly elevated spot. He'd stopped along the way to pick up sandwiches and cold drinks, and even found an old blanket in the trunk of his brand-new Buick convertible. He spread the blanket out under a wide-branched oak and motioned for her to have a seat.

"At your service, milady," he said with an exaggerated bow. "But only if I can join you, of course."

Mazie laughed. "I wouldn't have it any other way." Folding her legs beneath her, she sat down gracefully and patted the spot next to her. "How about right here?"

"Looks just right to me," he said, dropping down beside her with the bag of food and drinks in his hand. "So what do you think? Are you surprised?"

"Absolutely. Though I shouldn't be. You are without doubt the biggest romantic who ever lived. You've surprised me before, you surprised me today, and you will no doubt continue to surprise me in the future."

Edward's heart warmed at her words. Did he dare read a promise into them? Maybe. But he had vowed not to push her, so he would keep his hopes for the future to himself ... at least for now.

"So how's Mimi today?" he asked, determined to keep the conversation on safe ground as he unwrapped their sandwiches. "She seemed in great spirits at dinner last night."

"She's always in great spirits when you're around." Mazie smiled and took a sandwich from his outstretched hand, her fingers sending sparks through his own as they touched. "You know how she feels about you."

Edward nodded. "I do. And it never ceases to amaze me."

"Why in the world would you say that?"

"Well, she is from the deep South, you know. And she grew up there before the Civil Rights movement when things were ... different. You and I would never have been able to have a safe relationship in those days. It was even illegal in some places."

Mazie dropped her eyes before raising them again. "You're right. But if there's one thing I've learned about my great-grandmother, it's that she doesn't have a prejudiced bone in her body. She likes people, period. And she judges them accordingly."

"Good thing for me," Edward said. "Our relationship could be a lot more ... complicated ... if she were a different type of person, with different ... values."

Mazie nodded. "That's for sure. But, thankfully, she's not."

Edward took her free hand then and said, "Let's pray, so we can eat." She closed her eyes, and he offered a word of thanks before taking a bite.

"Turkey," Mazie said, smiling as she, too, took her first taste. "My favorite."

"I know that," Edward said. "That deli has every kind of sandwich you can imagine, but I knew you'd want turkey. They also have tuna, so we'll stop by there on the way back to the office and pick one up for Mimi."

"You think of everything, don't you?"

Edward grinned. "I try. Besides, I want to stay on Mimi's good side."

Mazie laughed. "I don't think there's anything you could do or not do to jeopardize that. She adores you."

"The feeling is mutual."

"By the way," Mazie said, pulling a piece of crust from her sandwich and popping it in her mouth, "Mimi showed me something last night."

Edward raised his eyebrows. "What was it?"

"A quilt. It was in her cedar chest, the place where she keeps all her treasures. I've never even been allowed to peek in there before, but she asked me to open it last night and get the quilt out." She paused before continuing. "She said she's giving it to me because she thinks the story behind it will mean something to me."

"Story?" He lifted his eyebrows. "What kind of story?"

"Mimi called it the Moses quilt because it was based on the life of Harriet Tubman."

Edward nodded. "Ah, the Moses of her people."

"Exactly. She said the story would take a while to tell, but she started with one of the patches in the middle, a small cradle that represented Harriet's earliest years as a slave."

As Mazie related her great-grandmother's tale of those first years, a cloud passed over the sun, and Edward shivered. This was just a little too close to home. And yet he was fascinated. Though he'd heard of Harriet Tubman, he'd spent his entire life in the Bay Area, scarcely setting foot in the South, and encountering very little in the way of prejudice or racism. Consequently, he'd never thought much about the famous woman nor studied the details of her life. Now he wondered if he might have missed something by not doing so.

CHAPTER FOUR

By the time evening rolled around, Mazie couldn't wait to clean up the dinner dishes and head for Mimi's room, where she hoped to catch another story about the Moses quilt. When she walked in and found her great-grandmother already in bed with her eyes closed, her heart sank. Though the quilt still rested on the chair beside the bed, it was obvious Mazie was too late. Her mother had taken care of Mimi for the night, and the stories would have to wait.

She turned to go but stopped at the sound of Mimi's voice.

"I'm not asleep, child. Just resting my eyes. I've been waiting for you."

Mazie smiled and returned to her spot on the chair, carefully lifting the quilt before she sat down and then laying it on the bed beside Mimi. "I'm glad. I was hoping you'd be up to sharing another part of the story with me."

Mimi's eyes were open now, and she smiled. "I will," she said, "but not about Harriet tonight. I want to tell you about the quilt itself."

"That's interesting," Mazie commented, "because Edward asked me about it today at lunch. He wondered where it came from and how you got it."

Mimi smiled, and her faded eyes took on a dreamy shine. "Do you remember the summer you spent with me and your aunt and uncle down in Prattville?"

"Of course, I do. It was one of the best summers of my life. How could I ever forget?"

Mimi nodded. "The hottest summer you ever spent too, wasn't it?"

Mazie laughed. "It sure was. I thought I'd melt right into the ground when we walked out of that Selma airport. If you hadn't gotten me moved from that horrible attic bedroom to the front porch, I wouldn't have slept a wink the entire time I was there."

"Maybe. Or maybe you would've gotten used to the heat."

When Mazie opened her mouth to protest, Mimi waved her away. "Never mind. It doesn't matter. The important thing is that you were in Prattville, Alabama, just a hop, skip, and jump from Gee's Bend. Do you remember my mentioning Gee's Bend while you were there?"

Mazie shook her head. "I'm afraid I don't, Mimi. Should I?"

Mimi sighed. "I suppose I shouldn't be surprised. I wanted to take you there before you went home, but you know I didn't drive, even then, and I couldn't convince your aunt and uncle to take us. They never understood the attraction or significance of that place. They'd rather run off and live in some foreign country no one has ever heard of. Costa Rica. Humph."

Mazie swallowed a smile and waited. She knew Mimi would share her story when she was good and ready—and not before.

"Anyway," she said, "Gee's Bend is a little horseshoe-shaped turn in the Alabama River. Nearly everyone in Gee's

Bend lives in the tiny towns of Rehoboth or Boykin. I doubt there's a thousand people between the two places, but then again, it may have grown a bit since I was last there."

The old woman paused, and her eyes fluttered. Mazie hoped she wasn't drifting off, particularly since she hadn't yet told her anything concrete to help explain the quilt's origin or what it had to do with a faraway place known as Gee's Bend.

Mimi opened her eyes and smiled. "I was just remembering how much I enjoyed my trips to Gee's Bend, one in particular. It wasn't long after my own great-grandma died. It was she who introduced me to the Gee's Bend quilts, you know, and so when she died I decided to go back there for another visit. That's when I came across this beautiful quilt, and I just knew I couldn't go home without it."

Ah, now they were getting somewhere. Mazie sat up straighter.

"That's why I wanted so much to take you there. Not just because of the Moses quilt but to meet the Gee's Bend quilters themselves." She shook her head. "Those ladies are a legend, that's for sure, with one generation teaching the next. Been making quilts for a hundred years or more. Famous for them, and they should be. Some of those women started making quilts when they were young girls, and by the time they died, they'd made more than most of us could count. But it was more than just turning out a lot of pretty quilts that earned a few extra dollars for their families. Getting together to work on those quilts was the center of the women's social life there in Gee's Bend. It bonded them together in a special way and gave them a sense of pride about living in that tiny little bend in the river—especially once they were discovered and their work started making its way out into the rest of the world."

"Are you saying these quilts have become famous, Mimi?"

"Maybe not famous to everyone," Mimi said. "After all, you never heard of them. But people who like and appreciate that sort of thing have banded together to help preserve the work they do there. Now people go there not just to buy quilts but to see the ladies who make them."

Mazie felt her eyes widen. "No kidding? Now I'm really wishing we'd gone there together when I was in Prattville."

Mimi smiled. "It's never too late, child. Maybe one of these days, after I've gone on to glory too, you could go back there and visit for both of us." She held up her hand. "I know what you're going to say. You'd want me to go with you." She shook her head again. "I'm too old, Mazie girl. It nearly killed me to move out here a few years ago, and I'm in worse shape now. No, I could never make the trip. But you could. And I hope one day you will." She smiled. "Maybe you could even take that handsome beau of yours along."

Mazie fought tears at the reminder her great-grandmother wouldn't be around much longer. She knew that, of course, and she knew too that Mimi had a strong faith in where she would go the minute she breathed her last. That was a great comfort to Mazie, but it didn't lessen the pain at the thought of her impending death. As for Mimi's reference to Mazie's making the trip to Gee's Bend and taking Edward with her, Mazie chose to ignore the remark entirely.

"I'm feeling a bit tired now," Mimi said then, her eyes fluttering once again. "Now that you know where the quilt came from, I think we'll stop for the night. I'll tell you more about the amazing Harriet Tubman tomorrow—if you're still interested, that is."

"Of course, I am, Mimi," Mazie said. "But ... just one quick question for tonight."

Mimi opened one eye and stared at her. Mazie took that as permission to ask her question.

"After you bought the quilt, did you ever go back to Gee's Bend? And did you buy it from the lady who made it?"

Mimi smiled. "Yes, and yes. And it was during our second meeting that she filled me in on more of the quilt's story, which I will gladly pass on to you. Now, do me a favor and turn out the light, will you? My eyes are quite heavy, and I think I just might be able to sleep tonight for a change."

The morning sky had scarcely begun to streak with gray light as Lilly sat at the kitchen table, sipping her coffee and munching a piece of toast while she read her Bible. She didn't have an appointment until nine and could have slept in a bit longer, but she enjoyed the peacefulness of early morning, plus it was the only time she had during the day to meditate on the Scriptures and to pray. Since being widowed nearly two decades earlier, Lilly had learned to depend on God as her Husband—Provider, Protector, and Partner. She wouldn't dream of starting her day without first spending time with him.

"Morning, Mom."

Lilly lifted her head and blinked in surprise. She hadn't heard Mazie's approach, but then she hadn't really been listening. Her mind had been elsewhere, and she did her best to pull it back now.

"Good morning, sweetheart," she said, smiling up at her daughter and marveling at what a lovely young woman Mazie had become. Her dark eyes were wide and bright, her lips full, with her dark hair framing an oval face with a flawless olive complexion. Even more beautiful was Mazie's sweet and generous spirit, and Lilly never ceased to thank God for such a fine daughter.

"I woke up early and smelled the coffee," Mazie said, heading for the carafe on the counter. "I couldn't resist."

"I'm glad," Lilly said. "We don't get much time to chat these days. And I have plenty of time before I have to go to work."

Mazie filled a mug and joined her mother at the table. "I didn't mean to interrupt your prayer time," she said, nodding toward the open Bible on the table.

Lilly smiled. "That's all right. The Father and I have had a nice conversation already this morning. I'm sure He won't mind if you join us."

Mazie smiled. "I wonder sometimes if I'll ever have as close a relationship with God as you do. I hope so."

"If that's the desire of your heart," Lilly said, "then God will see to it that you do."

"I'm sure you're right." Mazie's forehead drew together in a frown. "Mom, has Mimi ever told you the story of the Gee's Bend quilters?"

Lilly raised her eyebrows. "She's mentioned them, yes, though she hasn't told me an actual story that I can remember. Why?"

"She had me get her quilt out of the cedar chest a couple of days ago, and she's been telling me the story behind it."

Lilly nodded. "I wondered when I saw the quilt on the chair beside her bed. I've never seen it before, so I figured something special was going on."

"Don't you think it's a little strange she'd have me get it out, and tell me the story behind it, rather than you? You're her granddaughter, after all. I'm another generation removed."

"You're her namesake." Lilly smiled. "Ever since that summer you spent with her back in Prattville, you've been her favorite, you know."

"Oh, Mom, I'm sure that's not true. She has other grandkids and great-grandkids besides me. She just happens to be living with us, that's all."

"Maybe. But I think it's more than that."

"But ..." Mazie hesitated before continuing. "But she said she wants to give the quilt to me. That doesn't seem right somehow. I mean, shouldn't it go to you instead?"

Lilly laid a hand on Mazie's. "Honey, Mimi knows what she's doing. If she wants you to have that quilt, then she has her reasons. Don't question it. Just learn all you can about it and then appreciate it. When Mimi's gone, it will mean a lot to you."

Mazie nodded. "I've been thinking about that. I know she's getting old, and I see how much frailer she is all the time. I hate to even think about her being gone, but I know she will be ... soon. And yes, that quilt will mean a lot to me, of course."

"Good. Then just focus on that and don't worry about whether it seems fair she gives it to you instead of me or someone else. If Mom were still alive, she might have given it to her—they were close. And I know it broke her heart when her daughter died ahead of her." Lilly's voice cracked, and she cleared her throat before continuing. "Mazie, it's Mimi's quilt, and if she wants you to have it, she has her reasons. Just accept it gracefully."

Mazie nodded. "I will, Mom. Thanks. And I'm really looking forward to learning the rest of the story behind it."

Edward was at the office early, going over some briefs, when Tracy arrived.

"Hey, big brother," she called when she spotted his door open. She wandered into his office as he looked up.

"Hey, yourself," he said. "You're here early."

Tracy laughed. "Me? Sure, I came in to clear up some things before the phones start ringing. But I see you beat me to it. Something major going on?"

He shook his head. "Nah. Just want to stay caught up in case I can convince Mazie to go out to dinner and a show with me tonight. I'd like to sneak out a little early for that if she can make it."

"And why wouldn't she be able to? She's not working right now, is she?"

"Not until late August when she starts her first teaching position."

"That's what I thought." Tracy smiled and sat down across from Edward. "She'll make a great teacher. I've watched her around some of the kids at church, and she's a natural."

"Exactly." He grinned. "All the more reason she'd be a great mom too."

Tracy's nearly black eyes danced. "You have really got it bad, Edward James Clayton. Why in the world don't you just kidnap that girl and run off somewhere and marry her?"

"You think I don't want to? Trust me, there's nothing I'd like better. Well, maybe not the kidnapping part, but marriage? Oh, yeah. In a heartbeat."

"So what's the hold up?"

He shrugged. "I wish I knew. We get along great, and I know she's not seeing anyone else. But every time I bring up the M word, she nearly cuts and runs." He shook his head. "What am I doing wrong, Sis?"

Tracy reached across the desk and took one of his hands. "Nothing. Absolutely nothing." She hesitated. "It makes me wonder if …"

Her voice trailed off, and Edward knew exactly what she was thinking. The suspicion had niggled at his own mind lately, though he did his best to dismiss it. He and Mazie had discussed that very concern more than once, ever since it became apparent that their relationship could be heading in a permanent direction. Mazie had assured him it wasn't even an issue, at least so far as she or her family were concerned, but there were moments when Edward wasn't so sure.

"I want to say that can't be it," Edward said, knowing his sister knew exactly what he meant. "But then I ask myself, what else can it be?"

Tracy nodded. "What else, indeed? Mama worries about it and thinks it could be a problem, but this is the twenty-first century, for heaven's sake. It's not like we're still banned from sitting at the counter at the corner drugstore or have to sit at the back of the bus."

"Laws have changed, Tracy. But there are always a few hearts and minds that refuse to."

"Sure," Tracy agreed. "But I just can't believe Mazie fits into that category. Unless …"

"Unless?"

"Unless she just doesn't realize it … or can't bring herself to admit it. Do you think that's possible?"

Edward sighed. "I don't want to think it. I want to believe there's another explanation. But right now, I just can't come up with one. And apparently, neither can she."

CHAPTER FIVE

When Edward called and invited Mazie to dinner and a show that night, she accepted before realizing that meant she wouldn't be around to hear another installment of Mimi's quilt story. Had the story really become so important to her that she regretted having made a date to go out with the man she loved?

Loved. There was that word again. Did she really love Edward? *Could* she love him ... or anyone, for that matter? At times, she questioned if she even understood the word. And yet, after meeting Edward through his sister, Tracy, whom Mazie knew from a community food bank where they both volunteered, and subsequently sharing a relationship with him for more than two years, she couldn't imagine her life without him.

Then why don't I just say yes? Why not agree to marry him? It's not like we'd have to rush into anything. We could have a lengthy engagement—at least until next summer. I could get a year of teaching under my belt, and we could decide things like how big a wedding we'd want, where we want to live ...

She sighed as she washed up the dishes from the lunch she'd just shared with Mimi. One of the greatest questions in her mind was how in the world Edward could love her in the first place. *Not to mention, being so patient with me. I must be the flakiest girl on the planet. What kind of teacher will I be? Don't young, impressionable students need someone more stable than me?*

She shook her head. *Of course they do. What makes me think I'll be a good teacher when I can't even make a commitment to marry the finest man who ever lived?*

"Mazie?"

The faint voice scarcely registered over the running water, as Mazie rinsed the last of the silverware and stuck it in the dishwasher. She shut off the faucet, dried her hands on the towel, and headed for the hallway.

"Coming, Mimi," she called.

She opened the bedroom door and was pleased to see her great-grandmother sitting up in bed, leaning against a stack of pillows. For once, the TV was off.

"Not watching your programs today?" Mazie asked, stepping into the room.

"I was about to," Mimi said, "but then I thought you might have time to listen to another part of the quilt story."

Mazie smiled. "Your timing couldn't be better. Edward called earlier and invited me out to dinner and a movie tonight. Mom will be home by then, so I knew you'd be all right, and I accepted. The only problem was I was disappointed I'd miss out on hearing more about Harriet Tubman's story."

"Well, there you have it," Mimi said, smiling and nodding as she pointed at the chair. "God knew you needed another installment of the story before this evening. Television can wait. Have a seat, child, and I'll tell you as much as I can before I get too sleepy. You know how I like my afternoon nap, with or without the TV."

Mazie chuckled and sat down. "I sure do, Mimi. I've come in many times and found you snoozing while the TV blared away."

Mimi wrinkled her forehead. "Are you trying to say I'm deaf? Do I disturb you and your mother by playing the TV too loud? Because if I do, I can certainly turn it down, you know."

"Oh, no, Mimi," Mazie said quickly. "That's not what I meant at all. You don't bother us one bit with the TV. You just play it as loud as you like." She smiled and patted the old woman's hand, watching to see her face relax. It did, and Mazie breathed a silent sigh of relief. The last thing she wanted was to make the dear lady feel she was a burden in any way.

"All right, then," Mimi said, relaxing against the pillows. "Let me see now. We've talked about Harriet's birth and earliest years, and we've also talked about the Gee's Bend quilters." She shot a squinted glance in Mazie's direction. "And I've told you I think you should consider going there one day, after I'm gone, of course."

"Mimi, I—"

The old woman raised a gnarled finger and waggled it at her great-granddaughter. "I know what you're going to say, and I don't want to hear it. We've already had this discussion. It's time to move on with the story."

Mazie knew when to zip her lip. She nodded and waited.

"I'm not sure we started at the beginning when I told you about Harriet's birth." Mimi glanced toward the ceiling, as if trying to remember something, and then turned toward Mazie when she began to speak again.

"This part of the story is still about that first little patch I showed you—the cradle that signified Harriet's beginning. But none of us just starts from nowhere. We all had a beginning before we took our first breath on earth, and Harriet Tubman was no exception. It was Harriet's maternal grandmother, Modesty, who first arrived in the United States, compliments of a slave ship from Africa. No one seems to know anything about any of her other ancestors, but at least we know that much, and that's important, don't you think?"

Mazie nodded. She supposed it was true, though she was a bit hazy on why.

"When Harriet was a little girl, she was told by family members they were of the Ashanti lineage—which would now be Ghana—but like most information about Harriet, there's no real proof of that."

Ashanti. Mazie had heard the name but knew nothing about the people it represented. If someone like Harriet Tubman was descended from them, she imagined they must have been a noble people.

"Harriet's mama, often referred to as 'Rit,' may have been the daughter of a White man, though no one knows for sure. She worked as a cook for the Brodas family. Harriet's daddy, Ben, managed the timber work on the Thompson plantation, where he lived. They got married somewhere around 1808 and had nine recorded children, though most stories hold they had an even dozen."

The thought of so many children—whether nine or twelve—in one tiny, windowless, dirt-floored shanty once again sent Mazie's thoughts tumbling. Growing up as an only child in a comfortable, three-bedroom home overlooking a lush valley just miles from the Pacific Ocean made it nearly impossible for her to relate to anything even remotely close to what Harriet experienced as a child.

"It wasn't easy to hold a slave family together," Mimi said, "especially when the master was as uncaring and cruel as the ones Harriet and her family lived under. They thought nothing of splitting up husband and wife, parents and children, brothers and sisters, and sending them off to some faraway, unknown location, never to be seen or heard from again. It was heartbreaking and downright evil."

As lonely as it had been for Mazie growing up alone and wishing she had a sibling or two, she could only imagine how much worse it would be to have your family members sold off as part of a business deal or even on a personal whim. Mazie blinked back tears as she listened.

"But no matter how hard old Rit and Ben fought to hold their family together, three of their daughters were sold off by Master Brodas, and they never heard from or saw them again." Mimi shook her head, and Mazie thought the old woman was blinking away tears of her own.

"One day a trader from Georgia showed up at the Brodas Plantation and asked to buy the Tubmans' youngest son, Moses. Rit found out and hid that boy for a month, getting help from some of the other slaves and even some of the free Blacks who lived in the area. When the Georgia trader and Master Brodas showed up at Rit's door one day, demanding she turn over the boy, she declared, 'The first man that comes into my house, I will split his head open.'" Mimi chuckled, her laugh morphing into a cough that alarmed Mazie until the old woman regained her composure. "It's said that was the first time Master Brodas ever backed down in the face of a slave, but he gave up on trying to sell the boy. Many people believe that incident influenced Harriet into the belief that resistance was possible."

Mazie sat, wide-eyed, considering the courage it took for Harriet's mother to stand up to a man who could sell her, beat her, or even have her killed if he so desired. What else would she learn about Harriet Tubman and her amazing family before this story was over?

Apparently not much this afternoon, as Mimi's eyes were closed now, and her breathing was becoming deeper by the moment. Mazie pulled the covers up under her great-grandmother's chin and slipped out of the room.

Lilly had been swamped all day. She usually called Mazie to check in before lunchtime, but she'd had two walk-ins besides her usual clients that morning, and before she knew it her stomach was growling. She glanced at her watch and realized why.

Two o'clock! No wonder I'm hungry and need a break. Thank goodness I don't have any more scheduled customers for at least an hour.

She turned the sign that hung on the door to Closed and flipped the lock. Then she headed to the back room and pulled her lunch from the refrigerator.

It wouldn't be so bad if Sadie hadn't called in sick today. She could have picked up those walk-ins. She sighed. *Forgive me, Lord. I'm grateful for the business. You know I am. I just get so tired sometimes.*

By the time her food was ready, she'd opened a can of soda and plopped down at the corner table where she put her feet up on the extra chair. She considered kicking off her shoes but thought better of it. *As swollen as my feet are, I'd probably never get those shoes back on.* She tested the temperature of her casserole. *Too hot. Better let it cool a little.*

She took the opportunity to flip open her cell phone and punch in the speed dial digit for Mazie. It didn't take long for her to answer.

"Hey, Mom. I wondered why you didn't call earlier. You must be busy."

"Swamped. I'm just now sitting down to eat lunch. How's everything there?"

"Fine. Mimi's napping. What time do you think you'll be home?"

Lilly took another peek at her watch. If her three o'clock was on time, she'd be able to juggle that appointment with the one at three-thirty and get them both out by four-thirty. "If all goes well, I should be there by five. Why?"

She heard Mazie's hesitation before answering. "Well, I ... I'm thinking of going out to dinner and a movie with Edward. He asked me earlier, and I tentatively said yes, but I can cancel if you get held up there, or you're just too tired to take care of Mimi when you get home."

"I'll be fine," Lilly said. "What time do you need to leave?"

"Edward said he'd pick me up at six."

"Perfect. I'll swing by and pick up some Chinese takeout on the way home. You know how much your great-grandmother loves egg drop soup."

"Oh, that'll make her day," Mazie agreed, and Lilly could almost see the smile on her daughter's face. "It sounds so good I might even suggest Chinese food to Edward. He said I could pick where we go tonight."

Lilly nodded. "That young man is so good to you, Mazie, and so thoughtful. You know that, don't you?"

Another hesitation. "I do, Mom. Honest. He's the best."

"Good. I'd hate to see you lose him."

"So would I."

"All right, then. I'll see you this evening. And don't even think about canceling on Edward."

"Okay, Mom. See you later."

Lilly clicked off and turned her attention back to her lunch. She'd better get busy and eat so she'd be ready for her last two customers of the day. So long as no more last-minute walk-ins popped in, everything should go according to schedule.

She took a bite of food and then dug in her purse for her New Testament, which she carried with her everywhere. There was nothing she liked better than sharing a quiet meal with her Father. Besides, there were some issues involving her daughter and Edward that needed prayer. She just wished she was clearer on Mazie's reasons for hesitating to marry Edward. Somehow, deep down, Lilly sensed Mimi held the key. Was she finally going to present it to Mazie so the girl could be free?

"So it was your mom's idea to go Chinese tonight."

Mazie nodded. "She mentioned on the phone this afternoon she was going to stop by and pick some up on her way home. Mimi adores Chinese food, you know. And the more I thought about it, the better it sounded." She smiled, watching him closely. "And since you said I could choose the restaurant ..."

Edward returned her smile and reached across the table to take her free hand in his. "You didn't hear any arguments from me, did you?"

Still holding her chopsticks in the other hand, Mazie shook her head. "Not one. Sometimes I think you just might like Chinese food as much as Mimi and I do."

"Almost. Though you know I'll eat any kind of food imaginable, so long as I can share it with you."

Mazie's stomach tightened. A part of her responded positively to his affirmations of love for her, but another part pulled away, terrified of the implied commitments. Why couldn't she be like other women, particularly some of Mazie's best friends from college, who seemed to have no problem at all committing to relationships?

She stifled a sigh, not wanting to hurt Edward in any way but not wanting to encourage him either. It was like living her life on a balancing beam, and she was becoming exhausted by the constant effort.

"I appreciate that, you know I do," she said. "But next time, it's your choice."

Edward's smile widened, and his dark eyes danced. "Next time? I like the sound of that. When will that be? Tomorrow? The next day?"

Mazie laughed and shook her head. "You're impossible, you know that? You don't miss a beat." She shrugged. "Okay, day after tomorrow. Dinner at the restaurant of your choosing. How does that sound?"

Edward's face mirrored feigned disappointment as he sighed exaggeratedly. "It doesn't sound as good as tomorrow, but I guess I'll take it if that's the soonest you'll give me."

Mazie squeezed his hand. "I need to stay home tomorrow evening and give Mom a break with Mimi. But you know you're always welcome to drop by for potluck and a visit."

Edward's smile returned in full force. "Ah, now you're talking. You know I'll take you up on that offer. But forget potluck. What else does Mimi like besides Chinese? I'll bring it."

Mazie paused for a moment before answering. Mimi could be a bit finicky at times and her appetite had been waning lately, but she loved Edward and would no doubt eat anything he brought along. "How about some good old-fashioned cheeseburgers? She's always complaining we never fix those at home. I'll bet she'd love that."

"Cheeseburgers it is," he said. "And I know just the place. Remember the time I took you to that little hole-in-the-wall on Third Street? They aren't much for ambiance, but their food is great."

"I do remember, and yes, their burgers are the best. Now I'll be looking forward to them all day too."

"Perfect. Even if it's because of the food I'm bringing with me, I'd like to know you're spending the day anxiously awaiting my arrival."

"I will be." Mazie removed her hand from his then and returned to scooping fried rice into her mouth with her chopsticks. The realization Edward would be at the house the following evening made her wonder if he just might like to sit in on one of Mimi's installments of her Moses quilt story. If so, it would be interesting to see his reaction.

CHAPTER SIX

Less than twenty-four hours later, Mazie and Edward were gathered around Mimi's bed, everyone full of cheeseburgers and fries. Lilly had taken advantage of the free time and headed off for a good long soak in the tub. And Mazie knew her great-grandmother couldn't be happier to have two attentive listeners at her bedside.

"It's a beautiful quilt, isn't it?" Mimi had asked, holding it up by one corner in front of Edward. "Mazie, lift up the whole thing so he can see it better, will you?"

Mazie quickly obliged, and Edward oohed and aahed appropriately, though Mazie imagined he wasn't truly all that fascinated with the makings of a quilt. For a moment, she wondered if he'd ever even seen one. But then she remembered Edward's mother kept an old quilt folded and laid across the couch in her living room—one she said her own grandmother had made many years earlier.

"That's not just any old quilt," Mimi said as Mazie refolded it and laid it back on the bed beside her great-grandmother. "That's the Moses quilt, named after one of the bravest women who ever lived."

Edward nodded. "So I heard. Mazie's been telling me about the quilt and about your stories too. Harriet Tubman sounds like quite a heroine."

"I should say so," Mimi declared. "And let me tell you why. Harriet Tubman was raised by godly parents. Rit and Ben Ross may have been poverty-stricken and illiterate, as were Harriet and all her siblings, but they were rich in faith and devotion to God. Those two parents lived their faith every day in front of their children under the most difficult circumstances imaginable, and those children grew up knowing that Christianity was more than words. It's no wonder they all adopted their parents' faith as their own, and Harriet perhaps most of all."

Mimi lifted a corner of the quilt and held it out to Mazie. "Hold it up again, will you, child? I want to make sure Edward sees the cradle patch first, the one we already talked about, but I want you both to notice another patch now." She paused as Mazie opened the quilt and held it up. Mimi pointed. "See it? The patch right there, next to the cradle. It's a plain, simple cross, but it says more about Harriet Tubman than just about anything else on that quilt."

Mazie spotted the patch with the cross and noticed Edward too was giving it his attention as he sat beside her in a matching chair. He seemed enthralled with the quilt and Mimi's story so far, so Mazie laid the quilt back on the bed and leaned back, anxious to hear more about the former slave woman who had so inspired the ninety-three-year-old woman lying in the bed in front of them.

"If you want to understand this courageous woman," Mimi said, "then you have to first understand her great faith. There was no compromise when it came to her belief in God. From the earliest age, she was forced into a life that demanded complete trust in God if she were to survive. She understood that, and she practiced it daily. Combine that faith with a deep-seated desire to be free and to see her people free, and you'll get a glimpse of how one solitary woman—uneducated and without a dime to her name—accomplished so much for so many."

Mazie caught herself nodding and stopped. Quite obviously Harriet Tubman was a woman of faith and courage, the exact opposite of everything Mazie imagined herself to be. Could knowing more about this woman give her the inspiration she needed to become more like her? Mazie certainly hoped so.

"Harriet's parents set the example," Mimi said. "These were not people who prayed once in the morning and once at night. They talked to God all day long, and Harriet grew up doing the same. She also believed God talked to her. And when she heard from Him, she took His words seriously. Harriet came to believe early on that even if their bodies weren't their own, their spirits were. The cruelest master in the world couldn't take that from them. She committed her spirit to God, and she believed He would keep it safe."

Edward's hand snaked across the few inches between them as he grasped Mazie's in a firm grip and squeezed. She was glad he didn't let go as Mimi continued to speak.

"The difference between Harriet and her parents was Harriet began to dream of being physically free, of escaping slavery. When she voiced her dream to her mama and daddy, they got real nervous. They knew they could all be punished or even killed for talking about such things. But Harriet wasn't one to be discouraged."

Mimi sighed, and her eyes showed the first signs of a flutter. Mazie knew the old woman was growing weary. Was their story about to end for the evening?

"Next time, I will tell you about Harriet's very first attempt to help rescue a slave. She was still a child herself at the time, and she paid a great price, one that would haunt her for the rest of her life. But it was also one that strengthened her conviction to escape slavery and to help others do the same."

She smiled. "For now, though, my voice and my eyes are tired. I will have to say goodnight."

Mazie glanced at Edward, who looked disappointed just before he dropped her hand and bent closer to Mimi to kiss her cheek. "I understand, Mimi," he said, "and I appreciate what you've told us tonight. You've given me a lot to think about."

"Good," Mimi said. "Stories aren't just for entertainment, you know. Jesus told stories—parables, they were called then—and they were for challenging people right where they lived, changing hearts even if it hurt."

Mazie's own heart squeezed at the words. Is that what God was doing to her, challenging her right where she lived, changing her heart—even if it hurt?

She waited until Edward stepped back, giving her room to bend down and kiss Mimi as he had done. Then she followed him from the room, wondering what thoughts swirled through his mind as they headed down the hallway toward the kitchen. Somehow she imagined they included visions of the cross, sewn into the Moses quilt and so clearly epitomizing the life and courage of Harriet Tubman.

"So where are you taking Mazie for dinner tonight? You did say it's your turn to choose, right?"

Edward looked up from his paperwork and smiled at his sister. Tracy was a knockout, and he still couldn't figure out why guys weren't lined up outside their parents' house, waiting for a chance to see her, let alone ask her for a date. Then again, the very fact she had opted to live at home when she could easily have moved out on her own or shared an apartment with a friend said a lot about her inner beauty as well. The girl was a devoted Christian with a no-nonsense moral code she violated for no one. Edward decided she'd probably already scared off more guys with that code than other girls attracted over a lifetime.

"Yep, it is," he said. "My turn to choose where and what to eat. And you know what? I ran through all my favorite places in my head and decided I'd rather eat over at Mazie's."

Tracy raised her perfectly arched eyebrows. "Again? Weren't you just there last night?"

"Exactly. And exactly why I want to go there again."

Tracy squinted her eyes and moved from the doorway toward his desk, where she lowered herself into the seat directly across from him. "I don't get it. I know you like Mazie's family, but I also know you like having the girl to yourself. So what's up with going there for dinner two nights in a row?"

"It's Mimi." He grinned. "Seriously. Of course I'm going over there to see Mazie, and if that's all it was, then sure, I'd take her out somewhere romantic and private." He leaned forward. "But Mimi's got this quilt, and—"

"A quilt?" Tracy's voice had risen nearly an octave. "What are you talking about? You're not making any sense, big brother."

Edward chuckled. "I'm not even making sense to myself. I mean, who cares about a quilt, right? But this isn't just any quilt. It's called the Moses quilt, and it supposedly represents the life of Harriet Tubman."

Tracy's eyes nearly bugged out of her head. "Harriet Tubman? Really? I remember studying about her in school. She was an amazing woman."

Edward nodded. "The Moses of her people."

"*Our* people."

"Our people. True. I suppose that's why I'm so fascinated. Mimi's been telling bits and pieces of the story to Mazie, and last night I sat in on the part about Harriet's younger life and what a strong Christian she was. I guess I knew that somehow, but it hadn't really registered with me what a huge part of her life that was, and how impossible it would have been for her to be the courageous woman she was and accomplish all she did without that faith." He shook his head. "I have to tell you, Sis, it has really started me thinking about my own faith and how easily I take it for granted. And if I can get in on another installment of the Moses quilt story tonight, then I'm going to be there."

Tracy continued to watch him for a moment before answering. "Well then, it sounds to me like you made the right choice." She gave one quick, sharp nod. "Good for you. Go over there and listen to Mimi's story. And maybe you can pass it on to me some time."

"Glad to do it," Edward said, pleased at her reaction. "But I do have one question."

Her eyebrows rose again.

"I took cheeseburgers last night, and I know Mimi had Chinese food the night before. What should I take tonight?"

"Does she get heartburn?"

Edward frowned. "Mimi? I don't know. Why?"

"Call Mazie and ask her. If not, take pizza."

"You're saying that because it's your favorite food."

"Absolutely. You asked my opinion, and I gave it. Take it or leave it."

"I'll call Mazie right now," he said, reaching for the phone.

Mimi couldn't have been happier than when Mazie informed her Edward was coming back for supper that night.

"And you know why?" Mazie had asked.

Mimi shook her head. "I can't imagine, especially since you said it was his choice for where to go tonight. You'd think he'd want to take you somewhere a bit more romantic than our little kitchen."

Mazie grinned as if she were about to divulge the greatest secret ever. "Because he wants to come back and hear more of your story about the Moses quilt and Harriet Tubman."

Mimi was sure she'd felt herself beam even before Mazie saw it. What a fine young man that Edward Clayton was! And now he wanted to come over and spend an evening listening to an old woman's story.

She smiled to herself as she checked the clock on the wall above her TV. *He'll be here soon. And something tells me it's more than my charm that's got him coming back. Mazie too. She's a lot more interested in the Moses quilt story than I thought she'd be. You're up to something here, Lord, aren't You? Well, good. Somebody needs to get things stirred up here so all the secrets can get laid out in the open, once and for all, and then maybe these young people can get on with their lives. You and I both know mine is nearly done, leastwise here on this earth, and I'm ready when You are, Lord. It's all about the young people now, so give me the words, Father, please.*

She chuckled and finished her prayer out loud. "And would You please keep me awake a bit longer tonight? I'd really like to get through a nice long piece of this story without drifting off this time."

The muffled sounds of voices interrupted her, and she recognized Edward's smooth, deep laughter among them.

"He's here, Lord," she whispered.

Mazie had set a couple of chewable antacids on the stand next to her bed, and Mimi snatched them up now and popped them into her mouth, already anticipating the pepperoni pizza she'd been promised was coming, compliments of Edward. Then she relaxed against her pillows, waiting and knowing someone would come to take her into the kitchen in her wheelchair at any moment.

CHAPTER SEVEN

Mazie had enjoyed herself immensely, not just because of Edward's presence or even the exceptionally good pizza he'd brought for dinner but because she'd observed the absolute delight on her great-grandmother's face throughout the evening. The elderly woman's eyes had sparkled, even as she joked about eating her antacid appetizer before indulging in the spicy meal, and it was obvious she couldn't wait to get started on the Moses quilt story again.

"Mom, aren't you going to join us tonight?" Mazie asked as they cleared away the dishes and prepared to get Mimi into bed.

Lilly smiled as she rinsed the plates and placed them in the dishwasher. "Not tonight," she said. "I'm just too tired. But you and Edward can enjoy it." She smiled as Mazie returned from the table and handed the empty glasses to her mother. "I think it's right the two of you hear the story together."

Mazie cocked her head, studying her mother. What had she meant by that? Somehow, Mazie sensed it was more than just the possibility of their future relationship. Her mother was implying something, but Mazie couldn't quite grasp it. Did her mother even know what the story was about, or how it was supposed to affect the listeners, particularly herself and Edward? Mazie opened her mouth to ask but was interrupted as Edward came up behind her and placed his hands on her waist.

"I wheeled Mimi into her room," he said, grinning down at her as she turned her head to look up at him. "The rest is up to you."

She laughed and handed him a sponge and dishtowel. "All right then. You can stay here and help Mom, and I'll go get Mimi into her nightgown and under the covers, so we can go catch the next installment of her story before she gets too tired to tell it."

Edward kissed the top of her head, took the sponge and dishtowel from her, and turned toward Lilly as Mazie exited the room and headed down the hall toward Mimi's room. She wasn't in the least surprised to find her great-grandmother sitting in her chair, her eyes alight with anticipation when Mazie entered.

"I can't wait to tell you about Harriet's first experience in helping a slave escape," she said. "Edward is going to join us, isn't he?"

"Absolutely," Mazie assured her, retrieving a nightgown from a dresser drawer. "He wouldn't miss it. Remember, he gave up taking me out somewhere just so he could sit in on your storytelling tonight." She smiled down at her great-grandmother as she helped her unbutton her blouse. "To tell you the truth, I don't think he's going to miss a night until you've finished this entire Moses quilt story."

Mimi laughed. "Well, that's just fine with me. As far as I'm concerned, Edward could be here every day and every evening, and I'd be just fine with that." Her eyes narrowed but continued to twinkle. "Though it would make a lot more sense if you'd just marry that young man and get your own place."

Mazie felt a rush of heat to her cheeks but did her best to mask her feelings by teasing the old woman. "Why, Mimi, if I did that, you'd never see either one of us. You wouldn't want that, would you?"

"I know better," she answered. "You and Edward aren't the type to abandon your own family. And that's what I am. So, you'd still come around to visit. Besides, how much longer do you think I'm going to hang around on this earth anyway? Don't you think it's about time for me to move on? I have better things to do, you know."

Mazie laughed as she carefully slid the nightgown over Mimi's head. "You may have better things to do at some point," she conceded, "but we're not ready to let you go yet."

Mimi smiled at her. "I have a story to finish first, don't I?"

"You sure do," Mazie said. "And I'm going to go put a rush on those two in the kitchen, so I can get Edward in here and we can get on with it. I can't wait to hear the next installment." She got Mimi tucked into bed and headed for the door, turning back as she grabbed the door handle. "Now don't you start without us. Edward and I will be back in a flash."

By the time Mazie had rounded up Edward and escorted him into Mimi's room, the old lady was resting against the pillows, but her eyes fluttered open the moment the door opened.

"Ah, you're back," she said. "Pull up a couple of chairs. I want to show you another very special patch on the quilt, and then I'll tell you all about it."

Mazie sat down in the chair Edward got for her, and then watched him settle into his own. When Mimi offered a corner of the quilt to Mazie, she knew exactly what to do. Holding it up so they could see the various patches, Mimi once again pointed to one near the middle. "That piece right there, the one that looks like a heavy piece of lead. It represents a two-pound lead weight an overseer hurled at an escaping slave. It hit Harriet in the head and caused problems for the rest of her life."

Mazie set the quilt down, and Edward took her hand as they waited.

Mimi grew serious as she said, "I want you to do more than just listen to this story. I want you to close your eyes and picture it. This was no small event in this young slave girl's life. Many say it was the turning point, or at least a powerful impetus for her to pursue what God had already laid on her heart—to devote her life to rescuing as many slaves as possible, regardless of the cost."

Mazie cut a glance to the side and saw Edward close his eyes. She did the same, and then waited for Mimi's words to carry them back to a time and place that had never seemed relevant to her before but suddenly loomed large in front of her.

Thirteen-year-old Harriet was bone-weary, but no more so than usual. She'd spent the day laboring in the fields, as the distant hint of autumn teased the workers with a slightly cooler breeze than they'd experienced over the last months. Field work was difficult, but the sturdy young teenager was content to toil near her beloved father and brothers. Despite the backbreaking labor, she enjoyed being outside in the beautiful Maryland countryside. But one day, Harriet saw something that spurred her to take an action that would not only change the type of work she did over the next few years but would also drive her to pursue her dream of helping free as many slaves as possible.

Was it mere chance that caused Harriet to look up from her work when she did? Harriet never thought so. She believed it was an incident used by God to set her on the path He had purposed for her. And it was a slave named Jim who took the first step down that path, unaware Harriet would follow.

Whether it was a long-planned move or just an impulsive one, Jim glanced around the field that early evening and concluded no one was watching him. Whether he intended to escape entirely or simply detour to the nearby store without permission is uncertain, but off toward the store he ran. Jim was wrong, however, when he thought no one was watching. Harriet spotted him slipping away from the fields, and her heart nearly froze in place when she saw Barrett, the overseer, take off after him. She knew she could run faster than the overseer, so she decided to dash off through the fields and warn Jim before Barrett could get to him.

The young girl ran like the wind, but unfortunately she didn't get to Jim in time. When she arrived at the store and found the men already facing one another, Barrett ordered the sturdily built teenaged girl to help hold Jim so he could be whipped. Not only did Harriet refuse to do so, but she used her body to block the door so Jim could escape. Barrett was furious and snatched up a two-pound lead weight, hurling it at the escaping slave. He missed, and the weight slammed into Harriet's forehead, knocking her to the floor and fracturing her skull.

Harriet's mother, Rit, retrieved her severely injured daughter and took her back to their shanty, where she did her best to nurse her back to health, even though she had no medical assistance or supplies. The child lay on a bundle of rags in the corner of their tiny home, delirious and unable to recognize the people around her. But Rit wasn't about to give up. She continued to nurse her beloved daughter as best she could, and she prayed for her constantly.

The family's owner, however, had given up on her ever getting better. He decided she wasn't worth keeping and tried to sell her, but no one wanted to buy someone in such poor physical condition. Even her mental condition was in question at that point—as she lay in the corner, moaning and scarcely communicating with anyone.

Slowly, the girl's health and strength returned, as did her memory, though she was left with a permanent dent in her forehead. Most important, however, her spiritual strength and conviction grew, deepening her resolve to fight against slavery, at any cost. She also committed to pray for her master's conversion, believing that if Master Brodas became a true believer he wouldn't continue to be so cruel. "Oh, dear Lord, change that man's heart, and make him a Christian," she prayed, day and night, silently and out loud, every chance she got. "Oh, Lord, convert old master."

But even as she prayed and recuperated from her ordeal, she and her family faced another possible tragedy. Rumors around the plantation alerted the Ross family to the possibility that since Harriet was now feeling a bit better, Master Brodas was considering selling her and her brothers to a chain gang in the South. The very thought struck terror in Harriet's heart, as she knew once they were sold they would never see the rest of their family again— something she was simply not willing to accept.

That's when she altered her prayers. "Lord," she prayed now, "if you ain't never going to change that man's heart, kill him, Lord, and take him out of the way, so he won't do no more mischief." Not long after she began to pray in this way, the young girl heard the news that Brodas was indeed dead. "He died just as he had lived," she declared, "a wicked, bad man."

And yet the man's death troubled Harriet, for though she was relieved she and her brothers would not be sold to the chain gang, still she was concerned about her part in Brodas's demise. She wrestled with feelings of guilt until she finally concluded his death must have been God's will, which gave her some peace about the outcome.

The question now was, what would become of her with Master Brodas gone and Harriet still not strong enough to go back to work in the fields—a question that haunted not only Harriet but her family as well.

With images of a young Harriet Tubman, dent in her head and determination in her heart, still swirling in her mind, Mazie waited for Mimi to continue. After a moment, Edward squeezed her hand, and she opened her eyes. Mimi had obviously drifted off, no doubt exhausted from her extended storytelling time.

Quietly, Mazie and Edward got up from their seats, made sure Mimi was comfortable and tucked in, and exited the room—heading back toward the kitchen where Lilly sat, sipping a cup of tea. She glanced up and smiled as they entered.

"All done for the night?" she asked. "You were in there quite a while."

Mazie nodded. "Mimi really got into it this time. She went longer than usual. But wow, what a story."

"That's for sure," Edward agreed. "How did I not know that part of the story about Harriet Tubman? I mean, we studied her in school, but all I remember is the part she played in rescuing slaves. Even that's a bit fuzzy, I have to admit."

"Same with me," Mazie admitted. "Shows how much attention we paid in history class."

Edward chuckled. "I used to wonder why any of that mattered anyway. How did something that happened so long ago relate to me, here, in the modern world?" He lifted his eyebrows and shrugged his shoulders. "Now I'm wondering what else I missed when I was daydreaming and waiting for the bell to ring so I could escape."

"You're no different than the rest of us," Lilly said. "Somehow the lessons of history seem so far removed when we're young and full of ourselves." She smiled. "Maybe that's why we need someone like Mimi, who's so close to the end of her earthly life, to help us appreciate the past, so we can better understand the present and not fear the future."

Mazie was certain her mother was trying to tell her something, but she wasn't up to pursuing it now. "That tea looks good, Mom." She turned to Edward. "Would you like some?"

"If you're going to have some, sure."

She filled and put the kettle on the stove, while Edward joined Lilly at the table. Their amicable chatter warmed Mazie's heart, even as she wondered where the story of the Moses quilt would take them next. And how would it impact her relationship with Edward? For as surely as Harriet Tubman had known the master's death would somehow change her life, Mazie suspected change was in the offing for her as well.

CHAPTER EIGHT

Tracy sat on the family's wide front porch, enjoying the cool summer evening, only because she was wrapped in a snuggly blanket. Edward was always telling her how much Mazie's great-grandmother disliked the cold, damp weather of the Bay Area, and Tracy couldn't help but agree with her. The difference was Mimi had spent her entire life in the South until grudgingly moving in with Lilly and Mazie a few years ago, finding the stark contrast in weather only one of many difficult adjustments for one her age. Tracy, on the other hand, had lived in Langsdale her entire life, was scarcely in her mid-twenties, and should have no problem tolerating such weather. But no matter how she tried to convince herself of that fact, she still shivered each time she stepped outside into the morning fog.

Which will no doubt be out in force again tomorrow. She watched a lone car make its way toward her and then pass on by. *I'm probably the only native-born citizen of Langsdale who wraps up in a blanket in the summer. But winters are worse. I wouldn't even be sitting outside here if was past mid-October.*

Her parents had gone to bed early, leaving Tracy to watch TV alone. Finding nothing of any interest, despite her best efforts at channel surfing, she'd opted to grab a warm cover and park herself on the porch where she'd spent so many hours with her grandfather before he died. Pops had been her hero—not that she didn't dearly love her father, but her grandpa had doted on her and, unlike her busy parents, had always had time to listen to her problems and take her for a walk to the neighborhood grocery to buy her a crisp apple or, on occasion, an ice cream. Oh, how she missed those days!

Edward looks so much like Pops when he was young. She closed her eyes and remembered pictures of her handsome grandfather when he was courting her grandma. The wedding pictures were her favorite. Tracy thought they were the best-looking couple she'd ever seen, and the love that shone from their faces was something she dreamed of one day finding herself.

Is that possible, or am I just dreaming? She had asked herself that question more than once. It was obvious her parents cared for one another, but Tracy had never seen them look at each other the way Pops and Granny had done in their wedding pictures. Of course, that was long ago, and Granny had died so soon after they were married, leaving Pops to raise an infant son on his own. That baby had grown up to become Edward and Tracy's father, and Pops had parented him on his own all those years.

He never remarried. Tracy mused, thinking of the times she'd asked him why. "The kind of love I had with your grandmother only comes once in a lifetime," Pops had explained to her. "I wasn't about to settle for less."

And that's what had driven Tracy to reject her many suitors through her high school and college years. No one had ever affected her in a way that led her to believe they could share the sort of love her grandparents had known, however briefly. And she, like Pops, was determined to hold out for nothing less.

Edward says that's the way he feels about Mazie. He says he's loved her almost from the first time he saw her, and he can't imagine his life without her. I just hope she doesn't break his heart. But something is holding her back, that's for sure.

She shook her head. True love could no doubt be a glorious thing, but it was also complicated and full of heartbreaking possibilities. Maybe it would be just as well to do without it.

On that note, she rose to her feet, still bundled in her blanket, and headed back inside.

By the time Edward left Mazie's and headed home, he'd gotten his second wind and wasn't anywhere near ready to turn in for the night. Besides, what was waiting for him at home but an empty condo and a long, sleepless night? The weekend was upon them, and he didn't need to be at the office until Monday, so that meant no early rising the next morning. He probably should have tried harder to convince Mazie to go out with him once her mother and great-grandmother were both asleep, but she too had seemed tired, so he'd kissed her goodnight and told her he'd call her the next day.

Now what? The car seemed to have a mind of its own— as he found himself aiming toward his parents' place. But his dad would be exhausted after a busy week at the firm and had no doubt already turned in with Edward's mother. Still, Tracy might be up.

He turned onto their street and was pleased to see a light or two still on. Steering to the side of the road, he decided to take a chance and text his little sister. It took her less than a minute to respond: "Come on in, big brother. I'm sitting on the couch drinking hot chocolate and watching a lame movie. Want to join me?"

He laughed, clicked his phone shut, and pulled into the driveway behind Tracy's Toyota Prius. When she'd first bought the vehicle two years earlier, Edward had teased her incessantly about getting a "real car," but the idealistic young woman was determined to do her part to save the environment. All his arguments about the fallacies of global warming fell on deaf ears when it came to his sister, so he'd given up trying to convert her—so long as she understood he was never going to ride in her "wannabe car." She'd retorted that was fine with her, and they'd let the discussion die.

Edward used his key to let himself in and went straight to the family room. Sure enough, there was Tracy, curled up in a blanket on the couch, sipping from a steaming mug and sitting in front of the television.

"Hey," she said, smiling up at him, "you're just in time to watch the end of the stupidest movie ever made."

Edward laughed. "And why would I want to do that?"

Tracy shrugged. "Probably because you don't have anything better to do, or you wouldn't be over here." She leaned closer as he took a seat beside her. "So what happened? Did Mazie throw you out?"

He shook his head. "Now why would you say something like that? Mazie and I get along great."

"Um-hm." She rolled her eyes. "That's why you've been asking her to marry you for six months now, and she still hasn't said yes."

"Something tells me I've let you in on too much personal information about my life," Edward said, yanking a throw pillow out from behind his back so he could settle in more comfortably. "Maybe I should pull back on that in the future."

"Okay by me," Tracy said. "But I'm not your problem."

"You saying Mazie is?"

"I'm saying either Mazie's your problem … or she's got one. If she really loves you like you say she does, what's the holdup? It's not like you two haven't known each other long enough. You've been dating for more than two years now, right? You're gainfully employed, and she will be too come fall. So why wait? Don't you two want to be together? Or is she just not ready for commitments?"

Tracy's words stung his heart like a poisoned arrow, but he was determined not to let it show. "I don't want to rush her," Edward said. "We'll get married when the time is right."

"Or not." Tracy's dark eyes flicked up at him before darting away. "Sorry," she said. "That was uncalled for. I apologize."

"Apology accepted."

"It's just …" She raised her face to his. "I don't want to see my brother hurt, okay? And I can't help but wonder if Mazie isn't hanging back for the obvious reason."

Edward felt his chest tighten. This was a topic he was not willing to visit. "I'm not going there. Understood?"

Their eyes locked for a moment, and then, she looked away, refocusing on the television in front of her. "Fine," she said. "We won't go there."

"Thank you." He too turned his attention toward the TV, wondering if he shouldn't have just headed home to his quiet condo after all. It might be lonely there, particularly when he couldn't sleep and felt the need to hang out with someone, but at least he wouldn't have to deal with getting grilled about his love life.

Such as it is—immediately irritated with himself for letting Tracy's suspicions affect his mood. *Enough. Just watch the ending to the stupidest movie ever, and then you can graciously excuse yourself and go home. You can talk to Mazie tomorrow, and maybe even get another installment to the Moses quilt story before the weekend is over.*

The thought cheered him slightly, and he allowed the tension in his shoulders to roll away.

Mimi awoke in the early morning hours, her chest constricted and feeling like someone had parked a car there. She forced herself to breathe slowly, determined not to panic. No doubt she hadn't taken enough antacid to offset the spicy pizza the night before. When would she learn? Her doctor was always telling her she had to stay away from spicy foods, fried foods, heavy foods ...

Anything that tastes good. The pain in her chest eased slightly. *What's the point? At ninety-three, shouldn't I be allowed to eat what I want? Of course, then I have to pay the price ... like I am right now. Still, who wants to live five more years if all I can eat is pudding and oatmeal? It's not like I don't know where I'm going once I breathe my last—and not like I'm not anxious to get there.*

She continued to breathe slowly as she reached into the drawer of her nightstand and pulled out the antacids. *A couple more can't hurt. And who knows? Maybe they'll help.* She popped them in her mouth and let them dissolve, since her teeth were soaking in a container in the bathroom. Meanwhile, to take her mind off the continuing pain, she clicked the remote and watched her TV screen come to life. She doubted there'd be much on at this hour, but maybe a rerun of some old sitcom ... or perhaps a good Christian show. She'd been awake at this hour before and knew there was at least one Christian channel that stayed on all night.

Punching her way through the lineup, she finally found what she was looking for and settled in to listen to the gray-haired man with the lined face and powerful voice. She'd heard him many times and didn't always agree with everything he said, but she knew he loved the Lord, and that was all that really mattered to her.

The thought turned her mind back to Harriet Tubman, a woman who had little or no religious teaching or training other than the Bible verses her mother had taught her. And yet the young woman's faith was rock solid.

"You had a purpose for her, Lord," she whispered. "And there was no way her lack of education or money or even her freedom could stop that purpose from being fulfilled." She smiled. "That comforts me, Father. I want to know I've fulfilled every purpose You have for me while I'm here, but when I'm done, would You please just take me on home? I'd surely appreciate it, Lord."

The last of the pain in her chest ebbed away, and Mimi breathed easier as she listened to the TV preacher working his way through the third chapter of the gospel of John. Mimi had heard similar teachings more times than she could count through the years, but she never tired of hearing them again. Besides, even if she didn't learn anything new from the man's teaching, someone else might be watching and hearing about Jesus and Nicodemus for the very first time.

Mimi smiled and closed her eyes, praying for God to use the preacher's words to bring a sinner into the fold or to encourage a lonely soul or to heal a broken relationship. If she'd learned anything in her ninety-three years of life, it was that with God, anything was possible.

CHAPTER NINE

Saturdays were Lilly's busiest days at the salon. While nearly everyone else on the planet was sleeping in, she was up earlier than usual, preparing for a long but profitable day.

"And you know I need one of those, Lord," she prayed softly as she applied a touch of makeup. "I've had so many unexpected expenses at the shop lately. And now that Mazie's done with school, those student loans are going to need to be paid." She sighed. "I know. She said she's going to take care of that herself when she starts teaching in the fall. But she is my daughter, after all—my *only* daughter—and I really should help with those expenses."

She thought of Edward then, and how different her child's life would be from her own if Mazie and Edward got married. *Shame on you. That's hardly the reason you should want them to get married. Mazie should marry Edward because he's a fine young man, and he absolutely adores her. Deep down, I think Mazie feels the same about him. So why is she dragging her feet? Is it really the racial thing? I can't believe that. I certainly didn't raise her that way. Besides, if it were a racial issue, why would she go out with him in the first place?*

Something in the past perhaps, but what? Did Mazie somehow sense something even Lilly couldn't identify? But how could she?

Lilly shook her head and picked up a brush to tame her dark curls. *No, she couldn't possibly. Yet she needs to—if there truly is something. Even more reason for Mimi to finish telling her the story of the Moses quilt. Maybe that's how You'll lead Mazie to whatever the truth may be that she needs to know, Lord. If so, I just pray she can deal with whatever it is in a positive way.*

She set the brush down and gave herself one last check in the mirror. Not great, but presentable. It would have to do. She checked her watch. Just enough time to have a cup of coffee and read a couple of chapters from the Bible before heading out the door to start what would no doubt be a very long day.

Lilly eased out of her room and down the hall, careful not to wake the others, who it seemed were still sleeping soundly. Just to be sure, she cracked the door to Mimi's room and peeked inside. The woman was resting peacefully, her breathing deep and even. Lilly was about to close the door when she noticed the open container of antacids on top of the bedstand.

She frowned. *The pizza must have given her heartburn. Poor thing. She has to be so careful about what she eats these days.*

Once she had the coffee going, Lilly jotted a note to Mazie and set it on the table.

I think Mimi had some problems with heartburn last night. Keep a close eye on her, will you? If you need to leave for a while, just call someone from the caregiver list in the address book. I'd feel better if we didn't leave her alone just now.
Love, Mom

Confident she'd taken care of the details for the day, she settled down with a cup of fresh brew and her open Bible. Other than the sounds of a few chirping birds greeting the morning, the house was quiet, and she was soon lost in communication with the One who had loved her unconditionally and helped her immeasurably through both the pleasant and difficult years of her life. Lilly was more grateful than she could ever express.

Though it had taken him several hours of tossing and turning to finally fall asleep after watching the end of the movie and saying goodnight to Tracy, Edward was feeling optimistic about the day by the time he awoke.

Ten o'clock. I remember when I was a teenager and I thought Mom was getting me up early if she woke me at ten on Saturday. That was supposed to be my one sleep-in day all week. He grinned as he pulled himself from the bed. *Now I feel like the day's half gone.*

I guess that's what happens when you become a grown-up. He made his way to the bathroom, wondering if Mazie was awake yet. He decided to wait and call her after he'd showered. Maybe he could convince her to go out for a late breakfast or early lunch. Either would suit him just fine.

Tracy's words from the night before, about Mazie "hanging back for the obvious reason," nagged at his sense of well-being, but he shoved them away. It just didn't make sense. If that was the reason she hadn't agreed to marry him, why would she continue to see him at all?

No. It had to be something else, something to do with Mazie herself and not him. But whatever it was, he sure wished she'd get a handle on it so they could get on with their life.

The fear getting "a handle on it" might mean she would reject him entirely was something he simply wasn't willing to entertain. He pushed the thought from his mind and stepped under the warm spray of the shower, determined to wash away any negative thoughts and focus on having an enjoyable day with the woman he loved.

"And who loves me," he said out loud, for surely it was true. Mazie wasn't the type to live a lie. If she didn't care for him, she would have told him and moved on long ago. He would have to be patient a bit longer, and she would come around. And when she did, it would make all the waiting worthwhile.

"I'm sorry I couldn't get a caregiver on such short notice," Mazie said as she let Edward into the house. "Mom left me a note saying she wasn't comfortable leaving Mimi alone right now, and I agree. She's just so ... frail."

Edward's eyes were warm as he smiled down at her. "You never have to apologize to me for taking care of your great-grandmother. It's one of the many things I love about you."

She felt her cheeks warm, along with her heart, as he bent down to kiss her. How could she not love this man who so obviously and deeply loved her? And how could she not say yes to his proposal? Oh, how she wanted to ... if only she could quiet the doubts that nagged her. Where did they come from, and how could she get rid of them?

"So is Mimi up and around yet?"

Edward's question brought her back from her musings, and she nodded. "Yes. A couple of hours ago. I've got her bathed and dressed, and I promised to fix her breakfast right away." She frowned. "She said she wasn't very hungry, which used to be unusual for her, but lately, I notice it more and more. Still, I thought if I scrambled some eggs and offered her a bit of a change from her usual drab oatmeal she just might get her appetite back. And, of course, she'll perk up when she finds out you're here."

"Tell you what," Edward said, "I'll rustle up some bacon and get those eggs started. You bring Mimi out here, and we'll get her fired up for breakfast in no time."

"Oh, no, you're not going to come over here and do the cooking. You've been feeding us for the last few days. This one's on me." She smiled up at him, knowing he couldn't resist when she looked at him in a certain way. "Now you go on and get Mimi while I start cooking. If you behave, I might let you make the toast."

She watched his momentary resistance melt away. He kissed her once more before heading down the hallway toward Mimi's room. Still smiling, Mazie turned toward the refrigerator and opened the door, ready to get started.

CHAPTER TEN

Mimi felt better now that she'd slept a bit and had a bath. She still wasn't particularly hungry, but she imagined that was because she filled up on too much pizza the night before. *Not to mention all those antacids. Whoever said getting old isn't for sissies was right!*

But now she sat in her wheelchair at the kitchen table, doing her best to eat the scrambled eggs and bacon on the plate in front of her and enjoying the pleasant conversation between Mazie and Edward and herself.

What a blessing they include me in so much of their time. I can only imagine how much they would prefer to be off by themselves somewhere instead of spending the day with an old lady. She smiled as she caught a mutual glance that passed between the two. She could almost feel the sparks in the air.

"So, Mimi," Edward said then, laying his fork down on his now empty plate, "since we're all here, how about another installment of your story once you've finished eating?"

Ah, so that was the attraction—her storytelling. She knew, of course, that wasn't the only reason they were attentive to her. Mazie had been close to her since that first summer they met face-to-face back in Prattville, Alabama, when she was just a slip of a girl. And Edward? It had been much the same with him. The first time Mazie brought him home to meet her, Mimi knew he was a special young man—intelligent, compassionate, and obviously smitten with Mazie. As the relationship between the two had developed, Mimi had found herself cheering them on, hoping and praying they would move past any obstacles that might stand in their way of a full life together. That was still her prayer to this day.

"Well, now," she said, "that sounds like a fine idea—though I can't guarantee I won't nod off in the middle of telling it. I didn't sleep too well last night, you know, and I'm used to a nap in the afternoon. But I think I can stay awake long enough to get us started on the next installment. Just let me finish this delicious breakfast here, and then I'll let you prop me up on my pillows so I can get comfortable before we start." She lifted another forkful to her mouth, wondering just how much of the food she would have to consume before declaring herself too full to eat another bite. She was already looking forward to painting the next picture in the saga of Harriet Tubman and the Moses quilt. Mimi wondered what they would think of the patch with the rawhide switch on it.

Harriet was finally beginning to feel more like herself again, though she often wondered if she'd ever be free of the headaches that plagued her now, not to mention the fits of "sleeping sickness" that descended on her without warning. She worried she could drift off so suddenly, awakening later feeling confused and exhausted. She knew it was a result of having been hit in the head with the lead weight, but no one seemed to have any idea of what to do about it. And so, like so many other adverse circumstances and situations in Harriet's life, she accepted it and learned to live with it.

Still, Harriet wondered what would happen to her now. Master Brodas was dead, but that didn't mean she was free. She simply had a new master, and he could do what he wished with her. Harriet hoped he would consider her strong enough to send her back out into the fields to work with her daddy and brothers, but that was not to be the case. The alternative was not a pleasant one for the teenage girl. Her new master was young and had a guardian named Dr. Thompson, who was the one who decided her fate. As a result, she was hired out to a young couple named James and Susan Cook, weavers who lived about ten miles from the Brodas Plantation. Her primary job would be to care for their baby.

Harriet liked children and had grown up in a houseful of them. But caring for a baby was something else entirely, particularly when the parents expected Harriet to keep the child quiet and content at all times. If the little one so much as whimpered, the Cooks thought Harriet wasn't doing her job. The punishment was swift and cruel. In fact, "Miss Susan" punished Harriet regularly—and often just for good measure.

Harriet had arrived at the Cooks' place on her first day of work feeling nervous and uncertain, but she had no choice in the matter or any opportunity to learn her job before being thrust into it. That very first morning, as the teenager tried to hide her apprehensions, Miss Susan took a rawhide switch and beat Harriet in the face and neck—not once but four times—before the family had even sat down to breakfast.

These beatings became a regular morning ritual, one that continued throughout the day for anything and everything Miss Susan considered an infraction of the rules—rules that changed according to the woman's whims. Terrified, Harriet looked for ways to protect herself. She quickly came to understand there was no appealing to Miss Susan's mercy, so instead she began to wear as many layers of clothes as possible, particularly around her neck, which at least softened the blows to some extent. Harriet also learned if she cried and wailed, loudly and immediately, Miss Susan apparently concluded that she had done her job and would stop the punishment after a short time.

Harriet did her best to learn how to care for the Cooks' child, but her duties didn't stop there. Miss Susan insisted Harriet clean the house, though the girl had no training in how to do so. When she was instructed to dust the furniture, she did her best to oblige, but it was never good enough. As a result, the beatings continued.

One day, as the whip came down upon her neck and face, and Harriet was screaming as loudly as she could, Miss Susan's sister came in to check on all the commotion. When Miss Susan explained that Harriet wasn't doing her job correctly, the sister scolded her for punishing the child for something she'd never been taught to do. The sister showed Harriet how to perform some simple household chores to Miss Susan's specifications, and the situation improved slightly.

Whippings weren't the only sufferings Harriet endured at the hands of the Cooks. The couple fed her, but never enough to ease the gnawing in the girl's stomach. One day, Harriet spotted a bowl full of white sugar lumps sitting on the kitchen table, and though she knew better, her growling stomach drove her to take a chance.

"That sugar, right by me," she said later, "did look so nice ... so I just put my fingers in the sugar bowl to take one lump and maybe she heard me for she turned and saw me. The next minute she had the rawhide down. I gave one jump out of the door, and I saw that they came after me, but I just flew and they didn't catch me. I ran and I ran and I passed many a house, but I didn't dare to stop for they all knew my mistress and they would send me back."

Starved and terrified, the girl raced on until she found a pigpen, where she hid for five days. "The old sow would push me away when I tried to get her children's food," Harriet said, "and I was awfully afraid of her." Nearly starved, the girl finally decided she had nowhere else to go, so she returned to the Cooks' home and accepted her punishment so she could get some food, even if it wasn't enough.

At last, the Cooks decided Harriet just wasn't cut out for housework, so Mr. Cook assigned her to watch his muskrat traps. Harriet was relieved to be out of the house and away from Miss Susan, but she soon discovered her new assignment wasn't much of an improvement. Even when she caught a bad case of the measles, Mr. Cook insisted she wade out into the cold water to tend the traps. When she finally collapsed from a combination of exhaustion, illness, and malnutrition, the Cooks gave up on her and sent her back to the Brodas Plantation, where her faithful mother once again nursed her back to health.

Mazie brushed tears from her cheek with one hand, while Edward caressed her other hand with his thumb. How was it possible for one human being to treat another so cruelly? Mazie knew it happened, but to hear it in relation to a particular person—a teenage girl at that—and to realize how she suffered was almost more than she could absorb.

"How ... how did Harriet keep from becoming bitter?" she asked, as Mimi paused in her storytelling.

"The only way any of us can," Mimi said, her voice as weary as the expression on her pale face. "By staying close to God. Her relationship with him was at the center of everything Harriet Tubman ever did or said or believed. It's the reason she was able to accomplish all she did in her amazing lifetime."

"I know that has to be true," Mazie said, grabbing a tissue from the box on Mimi's nightstand and wiping her eyes. "But I'm just not sure I could do that, even with God's help."

Mimi's smile was weak. "I understand, and I often feel the same way. But then I remember the Scriptures promise we can do all things through Christ who strengthens us. There simply is no other way, child. Sadly, we just don't seem to learn or understand until we're put in a position where our own strength isn't enough. That's when we have to make the choice to turn toward God—or away from him. Thankfully, Harriet Tubman turned toward Him, time and time again, throughout her life, regardless of circumstances of suffering. And God used her mightily because of it." She shook her head. "I so admire that woman. Her faith is such a strong example to all of us ..."

A coughing fit seized Mimi, and by the time she'd quieted, Mazie knew there would be no more stories today. She and Edward tucked her in and kissed her on the forehead, thanked her for all she'd told them, and then slipped out of the room together. As Mazie closed the door behind her, she couldn't help but notice a stiffness in Edward's demeanor that wasn't there before.

CHAPTER ELEVEN

By midafternoon, Mimi was sleeping peacefully, and the caregiver service had responded with a call saying they had someone available to come over within the hour. Mazie accepted their offer and gave Edward the good news as soon as she hung up.

"Looks like we can go somewhere after all," she said. "The caregiver is coming over to stay with Mimi for a while. What do you think?"

"I think that's the best news I've heard in a while." Though Edward smiled and pulled her into his arms as they stood in the kitchen beside the sink, where they'd just finished cleaning up the dishes from their late breakfast, she again sensed the stiffness she'd noticed in Edward as they exited Mimi's room. Before she could ask him about it, he said, "Where would you like to go?"

Mazie filed her concern about Edward for later and considered his question. Her first reaction was that it didn't matter. She always found it easier to let Edward decide. But it was a nice day—sunny and a bit warmer than usual—and there was nothing she'd like better than a view of the coastline. She smiled up at him. "Are you up for a ride to the beach? We haven't done that in a while, and it seems like the perfect day for it."

"Absolutely. Does that mean you're going to wow me and everyone else by wearing a bathing suit and maybe even catching a few waves?"

Mazie laughed. "Not hardly. The sun may be out, but I know that water's got to be freezing. No way am I getting in that! But a nice drive and maybe a walk on the sand? Now that sounds like my kind of afternoon."

"Then that's the kind of afternoon you're going to get." He leaned down and kissed her. "I know just the place where we can take a nice long walk and maybe stop for some fish and chips or something."

"Now you're talking," she said. "You know that's one of my favorite meals."

"Mine too." He kissed her again. "So what are we going to do while we wait? This hugging and kissing stuff might work better if we were sitting on the couch."

"Oh, no you don't," she teased. "Before we leave, I have to sort out all Mimi's medicines for the week. It's my Saturday chore, you know, and I don't want Mom having to come home and do it. So if you want to make yourself useful, you can help me with that. I've got a list a mile long with all her medicines on it. Not only do we have to check to make sure everything is full for the week, but we need to check refill dates and see if it's time to call some of them in." She raised her eyebrows. "Of course, if that's too hard for you, you can go sit on the couch alone and take a nap while I do all the work."

Edward shook his head. "You drive a hard bargain, Mazie Hartford." He sighed. "Okay, fine. Get the list out, and let's get started. I want this all done before the caregiver gets here because once she does, I'm swooping you right out that door. You got that?"

She lifted her hand and gave him a mock salute. "Got it. Now let's get to work."

The day was even more perfect than she'd expected. The temperature hovered in the high seventies, with a light breeze off the ocean that tossed her dark, shoulder-length curls and cooled her bare shoulders just enough to keep her comfortable as they meandered their way along the damp, packed sand. They carried their shoes and held hands as they walked. Other couples passed them, some also walking hand-in-hand, some with arms around one another's waist, some not touching or even talking, but all leaving footprints in their wake.

Mazie thought about the footprints she and Edward left behind. She couldn't help but compare them to the footprints left behind by someone like Harriet Tubman. How many followed in Harriet's footsteps even now, inspired by her courage and her faith, her selfless life and powerful legacy? Would anyone ever follow in Mazie's footsteps, challenged by some honorable deed or sacrificial gift?

It was a question that bothered her more and more lately, particularly now she'd begun to listen to Mimi's story about the Moses quilt. Mazie had always thought she had a strong faith and, for the most part, modeled an exemplary Christian lifestyle. But did she? Was it enough to believe in and adhere to the basic tenets of the Christian faith? Or was God calling her to something more? Was He, in fact, calling all His people to something more? If so, how many truly responded?

"All right, what's going on in that beautiful head of yours?"

Mazie jerked her head up at the sound of Edward's words. Even with her sunglasses on, she squinted into the sunlight as she gazed up at him. They stopped walking and stood facing each other just as the cold foamy remnants of a wave reached far enough to wash across their bare feet.

Her first thought was to deny she'd been thinking about anything in particular, but that wouldn't be true. And the last thing she wanted between herself and Edward was anything less than the truth. The problem was that at times, she wasn't sure what that was.

"I was thinking about Mimi's stories."

Edward nodded. "So was I. It's hard not to. That Harriet Tubman was something else, wasn't she? I can't even begin to imagine what her life was like."

"It certainly wasn't easy. And it sure helps put ours in perspective, doesn't it? Just about the time I think I might have something to complain about, I only need to think about Harriet and the cruelty she endured." She shook her head. "It's mind-boggling—especially when you think thousands of other people lived in similar conditions— maybe even worse."

Edward's jaw twitched and his grip on Mazie's hand tightened. "People like mine."

Mazie swallowed, ignoring the foamy waves that teased their bare feet. "Yes. People like yours. Do your ... parents ever talk about it? About your ancestors, I mean?"

"Not really. Dad's been so successful in his practice, and none of us has ever really suffered much. But Pops used to bring it up occasionally."

"Your grandfather? I wish I'd known him."

Edward's strained countenance eased. "I wish you had too. He lived with us in his last years, and he died way too young. Lung cancer. It was a hard thing to watch."

"Did he ... smoke?"

"Sure. Not when he lived with us, of course. My mother would never allow it. But I did catch him sneaking one now and then outside, when he thought no one was around."

"Even after he knew he had cancer?"

Edward nodded. "Even then. I guess he figured it was too late. He was dying anyway."

Mazie sighed. "So ... how do you think he would have felt about me? About ... us?"

The slight hesitation told her Edward was choosing his words carefully. "He might have been uncomfortable with it at first. But once he got to know you, he would have loved you. Just like I do. Like my parents and Tracy do."

"Do you really think so? Not just that your grandpa would have loved me, but that your family does? Your mom and dad and ... Tracy?" She dropped her eyes for a moment before raising them again. "Because sometimes I wonder if Tracy really does ... not just love me, but ... accept me. Not that she isn't always great to me, because she is. And I know she's the one who first introduced us, though I doubt she thought we'd end up as a couple. Still ... sometimes I catch her looking at me, and I see questions in her eyes."

Edward lifted a hand and caressed her cheek. "Mazie, we all love you. There's no question of that. If you see any questions or doubts with Tracy, or even my parents or me, it's just because we see in you this hesitancy, this resistance to what seems so right. And to be honest, sweetheart, we just can't figure it out."

The loving truth of his words sliced through her heart like jagged lightning, and she commanded her knees not to buckle. If only she could deny his doubts, but how could she? It would be so much easier if she could at least identify them. Maybe then they could work through them together and finally get on with their life together.

"I ..." She struggled to voice her feelings, determined to push on and say the things she'd wanted to say for so very long. "I can only tell you that I love you, Edward. That much I know. What I don't know any more than you do is why I resist what my heart longs for—and that's to say yes to you—to be your wife. But until I can figure out what it is that stops me from doing that, I have to wait." She swallowed a sob. "And I have to keep asking you to wait too. I know it's not fair, and I worry I'll make you wait so long I'll lose you. But ... what else can I do? I have to be sure."

Slowly, tenderly, Edward pulled her against his chest. He kissed the top of her head and stroked her hair, though he didn't say a word as another wave lapped against their feet and ankles.

By the time the summer sun had set and the cool breezes tamped the temperature down, Edward and Mazie were once again gathered around Mimi's bed. Lilly had come home and shared a simple supper of soup and crackers with her grandmother and then gone to bed, exhausted from a long day on her feet and grateful for Mazie's offer to get Mimi settled in for the night.

Knowing Edward had come home with Mazie, Mimi had insisted they come back in for a brief portion of Harriet's story. "I want to finish what I was telling you yesterday," she explained. "There's just a bit more to that part of the story."

And so they sat with her now, the quilt lying on the bed next to the old woman, as Mazie tried to blot out the memory of the words she'd spoken to Edward at the beach—the words expressing her concern about losing him. He hadn't responded to them except to hold her and to continue with their walk. As he had when they listened to Mimi's stories earlier, he now held her hand quietly as they waited for the elderly woman to speak.

"Thanks to Old Rit's tender care of her daughter, Harriet recovered once again," Mimi said at last, "despite the awful treatment she'd received from the Cooks. But then, she was sent out once again as a housekeeper for a different woman, who treated her every bit as badly as Miss Susan had done. She whipped and cursed her and treated her worse than a dog, finally sending her back to her mother. And Harriet was glad of it, let me tell you. The amazing thing is as Harriet got older, she claimed to have no ill feelings toward her former masters. She said they just didn't know any better."

The old woman shook her head. "Once again, it has to have been her strong faith that gave her such a forgiving heart. That slave girl might not have been able to read, but she loved the Holy Scriptures. She listened to them every chance she got and committed many of them to memory. One of her favorites was Isaiah 16:3. 'Hide the fugitives, do not betray the refugees.' You know that verse had a powerful impact on her impressionable young heart. And she was known for praying nearly every waking moment of her life. Kept a running dialogue with God, she did—but always a humble one. Why, that illiterate slave girl even came up with her own songs of praise to the Almighty. I remember reading one that went something like this."

She closed her eyes as Mazie and Edward waited. After a few moments Mimi, eyes still shut, recited words that made Mazie's heart ache over their simplicity and depth.

"Dark and thorny is the path," Mimi intoned, "Where the pilgrim makes his way. But beyond this vale of sorrow lie the fields of endless days."

Mazie's admiration for the former slave continued to grow, along with her amazement at Harriet's response to her tormentors. Truly Mimi was right it had to be Harriet's great faith that sustained her and protected her from becoming bitter, even as her resolve grew to help find freedom for her people. There simply was no other explanation.

Mazie glanced at Edward, sensing his tension had returned. The twitch of his jaw assured her she was right.

"Eventually Harriet was allowed to return to work in the fields," Mimi said. "She often worked side by side with her daddy and brothers, and she was grateful to do so, despite the backbreaking labor. In the evenings, they sat together with some of the other slaves, swapping stories about their ancestors and how they had come over on slave ships. Harriet was a tenderhearted girl. Many a night she cried herself to sleep, thinking about what so many of her people had endured. Is it any wonder her resolve to set them free grew stronger amid her own suffering? It was all part of God's preparation for the great work He had for her in the future."

Mazie found herself nodding. Yes, it made perfect sense— for Harriet. But what about her? How had she ever suffered? She hadn't, and perhaps that was the problem. Maybe that was why her faith was so weak and her emotions so unsteady. It made her wonder just what sort of wife she'd be if indeed she agreed to marry Edward. Didn't he deserve better?

"I think she's asleep," Edward whispered, leaning near.

Mazie blinked and focused on Mimi. Edward was right. Mimi's eyes were shut, and her breathing indicated she'd drifted off. It was enough for tonight. They would move on to the next phase of Harriet's story tomorrow, after church, if Mimi was up to it.

CHAPTER TWELVE

Tracy didn't make a habit of attending any church other than the one in which she'd grown up and her family still attended. But her parents were out of town that weekend, enjoying a little "alone time," as her father called it, and Tracy knew Edward was planning to go to Mazie's church this weekend. He'd made a point of inviting Tracy to join them, and she'd turned him down, but now, she was having second thoughts.

It's so silly. She primped in front of the mirror, trying to match her earrings to the dress she'd finally chosen after trying on three others. *It's not like I'd be sitting alone at my own church. I know everybody there just like they were family.*

She wasn't convinced. For whatever reason, she felt drawn to call Edward and ask if the invitation was still open. At last, she gave in and dialed his cell phone.

"Hey, Sis," he answered. "What's up?"

"Nothing much. Just ... wondering if I could change my mind and join you and Mazie for church after all."

She could hear the smile in his voice. "Are you kidding? Of course you can. You know you're always welcome to come with us—anytime. And it's not like you haven't visited there a couple times before."

Tracy nodded. She knew that was true, and yet she'd seldom made the decision to join them, despite numerous invitations to do so. Deep down, she had to admit at least part of what she was feeling on this unusual morning was a desire to see Mazie and Edward together—at a church where just decades earlier, Edward would have been barred from worshipping. Something just wasn't right in that relationship, and she sure hoped the two of them would work through it soon.

"Should I meet you there?" she asked.

"That might be best. We'd come and get you, but Mimi moves pretty slow these days, so it'll take us awhile to get there even without stopping to pick you up."

"No problem. I'll probably get there a little ahead of you and meet you by the front doors."

"Sounds like a good plan to me." He chuckled. "I'll just look for the best-dressed lady on the church steps, and I know it'll be you."

Tracy smiled. Her brother had always teased her about what he considered her excessive attention to her looks, particularly when she insisted she was not interested in attracting any male attention. But she always wanted to look her best, whether at work or grabbing a burger downtown—but most of all when she went to the house of the Lord. Her parents had taught her and Edward too the importance of giving God your best, and she wasn't about to compromise on that teaching in any way—even if Mazie and her family did attend a church that didn't seem to care if people came in suits or blue jeans. She certainly hoped Edward wouldn't show up in the latter.

Mimi very nearly begged off from attending church that morning, but she knew if she did the others would stay home too, simply out of concern. And so she had allowed Mazie to help her dress and finally get maneuvered into the back seat of Lilly's car. With Edward sitting next to her and the other two ladies in the front, they all took off with a few moments to spare.

She tried to relax, leaning her head back and closing her eyes, smiling when she felt Edward's hand on top of hers. He was such a fine young man, and despite the fact that her ancestors would certainly not have agreed, Mimi hoped the two young people would one day soon find their way to a life together. *Don't kid yourself, old woman. If this isn't indeed a match made in heaven, then it is doomed to failure. Such a serious obstacle to overcome. Lord, only You! Only You...*

By the time they pulled into the church parking lot, Mimi had dozed off and found herself quite disoriented when she heard voices calling her name.

"Mimi, we're here. It's time for church now. You need to wake up, so we can get you inside."

Mimi opened her eyes and found Lilly gazing at her. The woman was leaning into the open door, patting her shoulder. "Are you awake now, Mimi?"

The old woman did her best to nod, though she would have liked nothing better than to close her eyes and drift right back to sleep. It seemed that's all she wanted to do lately. Even eating was becoming a bit of a chore. Breathing, however, seemed to be her biggest challenge.

She realized she was the only one left in the car, as Edward now appeared behind Lilly, pushing the wheelchair.

Mazie stood at his side. It seemed the three of them were going to get her out of that car and into church whether she cooperated or not, so she might as well do what she could to help.

"Yes, my dear," she said, speaking to Lilly, who still leaned close. "I'm awake. If you all can get me into that wheelchair, then I'm ready for church."

With a few deft movements, she was in the chair. Edward wheeled her toward the entrance while Lilly and Mazie walked alongside. As he pushed Mimi up the ramp, the old woman spotted a lovely, familiar face near the doorway.

Edward's sister, she thought, chasing her memory in search of the girl's name. *And dressed like a fashion plate. That peach-colored suit is stunning on her. But I do hope someone says her name soon, as I can't for the life of me remember it.*

"Tracy," Mazie said, breaking into a smile. "Edward said you were planning to meet us here. I'm so glad."

The two young women embraced, and Mimi was glad her great-granddaughter had worn a dress this morning. Though it didn't compare to Tracy's attire, it at least looked respectable. Mimi wondered if Tracy's presence was the reason Edward had shown up in a full suit and tie, rather than slacks and a nice shirt as he often did when he joined them for church.

It doesn't matter, she told herself. *The important thing is we're all here together, ready to worship the same God and Savior. And thank goodness, I now know the girl's name.*

She smiled up at Tracy, as the young woman leaned down to offer a hug and an air kiss on her cheek. *How much simpler it will all be when we are no longer trapped in these mortal bodies* "It's wonderful to see you again, Tracy. I'm so pleased you've joined us."

As the five of them entered the sanctuary together, Mimi did her best to breathe deeply, but the pain in her chest was becoming more pronounced with each passing day. The antacids she gulped more regularly now didn't seem to help much anymore, convincing her that time was running out. *I must finish the story of the Moses quilt quickly.* She sensed the need for both Edward and Mazie to hear the entire story before they learned the truth that must be faced if ever they were to find the common ground they needed for the building of their future together.

Mazie was surprised when Mimi insisted on telling more of Harriet's story that afternoon. Tracy had gone home after church, declining their invitation to join them for lunch. Then Mimi had begged off as well, saying she was simply too tired to sit through a meal at a restaurant. And so they had gone home and managed to get some soup down her before putting her to bed. She napped as the three of them sat around the kitchen table, sharing sandwiches and conversation until Lilly excused herself to check on her grandmother.

"She's awake," Lilly announced when returning to the kitchen. "And she asked that the two of you come in to see her."

Leaving Lilly to clean up what few dishes were left, the couple joined Mimi in her room, settling into what were becoming familiar spots around her bed.

"How are you feeling, Mimi?" Mazie asked. "You seemed a bit tired after church."

"Humph. I was a bit tired *before* church. By the time it was over, I was exhausted. But now I've had a nap, and I'm ready to tell you the next part of Harriet's story."

Mazie raised her eyebrows. "Are you sure? Because Edward and I don't want to push you if you're not feeling up to it. We can wait until another time."

Mimi reached a withered hand toward her, startling Mazie at the paper-thin feel of it when they connected. "My dear," Mimi said, "never wait for another time if something needs to be done now. Remember, God numbers our days, and only He knows if we will have another time ... or not."

Mazie felt her heart constrict. She'd been trying for days to shove away the thought that Mimi was failing, but now she knew it was true. She exchanged a quick, pained glance with Edward before forcing herself to smile and clasp Mimi's cold hand in her own.

"You're right, Mimi," she said. "Now is the perfect time. We'd love to hear more about this amazing woman and your wonderful Moses quilt."

With a faint smile, Mimi nodded and said, "Lift up the quilt. It's time to show you another patch."

Obediently, Mazie did so, and then waited.

"There," Mimi said, pointing to a square not far from the previous ones she'd shown them. "That patch with the two white bells on it. Do you see it?"

Mazie and Edward looked and then nodded. "I see it, Mimi," Mazie said, confirming her words by touching the square.

"I see it too," Edward added. He leaned closer and squinted his eyes. "And what's that image between the bells? It looks like ... like a broom."

Mimi laughed, lapsing into a brief coughing fit before continuing. "It most certainly is a broom. Surely you've heard of 'jumping the broom,' a ceremony practiced by most slaves in those days, haven't you?"

Mazie and Edward exchanged glances before turning their attention back to Mimi. "I suppose I have," Edward said, "though I never thought much about it. It had something to do with getting married, right?"

Mimi nodded. "Exactly. Though I'm a bit fuzzy on the origin of the practice, it seems the bride and groom would jump over a broomstick to seal their vows to one another." She chuckled, and Mazie was relieved she didn't start coughing again. "Many people, including Harriet's parents, thought the girl would never marry," Mimi said. "Most slave girls married in their mid-teens, but Harriet was still recovering from her head wound then, and a lot of people thought she was simple because of the problems it caused." She closed her eyes as a dreamy smile spread across her wrinkled face, taking several years off her age. "But then she met John Tubman ... and everything changed."

CHAPTER THIRTEEN

Harriet knew she wasn't the only one who had given up on her chances of getting married. Even her parents and most of her siblings assumed she was too old at twenty-three to attract a man, particularly since she didn't have the prettiest face on the plantation. But she was a hard worker, a woman of great faith, and she had a powerful singing voice. John Tubman, a liberated African American who always carried his "freedom papers" with him to prove he was no longer a slave, was also an observant man who didn't allow Harriet's qualities to escape his notice.

The two worked side by side for a man named John Stewart, a common practice in those days. For that very fact, freed Blacks made it a point to have their papers with them wherever they went so as not to be mistaken for slaves, even though both groups did nearly the same type of work.

The first time John Tubman spoke to Harriet, she was confused by his attentions. *Why would this handsome free man pay attention to me?* Her eyes widened and her heart raced as she searched for a proper response. She certainly didn't want to further the common misconception she was mentally defective, but she imagined her hesitant, stammering reply may have done just that.

Soon, however, Harriet could no longer deny the truth of John's interest in her. He sought her out whenever possible, and even joined her when she launched into song—which was a common occurrence for the young woman with the powerful voice. The two of them soon became a popular duet in the fields where they labored—not just in song but as a couple. When John Tubman asked Harriet to be his bride, she quickly and wholeheartedly accepted.

I'm gettin' married. Me, Harriet Ross. Who woulda thought it could ever happen? She dreamed of it throughout the backbreaking days of toiling in the fields. Her mind focused on it at the end of the day when she shared a meager meal with her family. And her heart embraced it as she lay on her back at night, waiting to drift off to sleep.

Finally, one day in 1844, in the presence of family and friends, both slave and free, Harriet Ross became Harriet Tubman. Though a simple ceremony, with no mention of "till death do us part" or "what God has joined together let not man put asunder," since Harriet was still a slave and could be sold or traded away by her master any time, Harriet's dreams came true and her singing took on a whole new level of joy.

The ecstatic young woman watched her new husband's every move throughout that monumental day, and she couldn't help but think of the bonus she'd been given in addition to a good-looking, charming husband, John Tubman was a free man who could also read and write. Though Harriet was illiterate, she greatly admired anyone with such skills and wondered how God might use it to help her fulfill her dream of being free herself—and of helping her people achieve that same freedom.

But for now, the thought of sleeping in her husband's arms that first night of their marriage was enough to keep her smiling and singing as she celebrated with those who had come to witness their wedding day.

Mazie listened, enthralled, but she couldn't help but notice Mimi's growing weakness. She was relieved when it appeared the old woman was winding down her story for the day.

"Are you ready to sleep now, Mimi?" she asked.

"Almost." She patted Mazie's hand. "Just a little more first. You see, though John was a free man, thanks to a stipulation in his former master's will, they still had to live in the slave quarters because of Harriet's status." She sighed. "And sadly, so far as anyone knows for certain, they never had any children. John, however, seemed much more satisfied with their simple life than Harriet. Her entire being still burned with the longing for freedom, but each time she suggested to her husband they make a run for the North, he discouraged her, even threatening to betray her if she tried it. John's attitude broke poor Harriet's heart, and she soon found herself wondering if she could stay with John, or if she would have to make the painful choice to leave him behind and try to escape on her own."

Mazie felt her eyes widen. "That must have been one of the hardest decisions anyone ever had to make," she said, aware of the crackling in the air between herself and Edward. What would she have done in Harriet's place? The question left her nearly breathless.

"Exactly," Mimi agreed. "Something for us all to consider, don't you think?"

Before Mazie or Edward could answer, Mimi's eyes closed, and she whispered, "I'm ready to sleep now, dear ones. Perhaps I'll have another story for you later this evening. Until then, you two go spend some time alone together, will you?"

"You heard her," Edward whispered, leaning near her ear as they made their way down the hall toward the kitchen. "She wants us to spend some time alone together. I think we should honor her wishes, don't you?"

Mazie tried to swallow her grin but couldn't. "That's awfully kind of you," she said. "I admire your willingness to oblige an elderly lady's request."

Edward's arm snaked around her waist, and he pulled her close. "Any time. Especially when that elderly lady is related to someone as beautiful as you."

Her cheeks warmed as she leaned against him. How he drew her—and how she wanted to push past her resistance to that drawing. Why couldn't she be more like Harriet Tubman, who jumped the broomstick with joy to marry a man who later threatened to turn her in if she tried to escape from slavery? Harriet was obviously an all-or-nothing kind of woman, a woman with a courageous and selfless heart— the opposite of Mazie Hartford, who couldn't make a simple commitment to marry the finest man she'd ever known.

"So where are we going to go?" Edward asked as they stepped into the kitchen.

Mazie stopped in front of him and looked up into his warm, dark eyes. "I'll have to make sure Mom doesn't mind staying with Mimi for a while," she said, doing her best to ignore the lump in her throat. "If she's okay with that, we can go anywhere you like."

Edward's smile was slow, lighting up his eyes as it spread across his face. "Anywhere?"

Uh-oh. She'd put her foot in it now. "Anywhere within reason," she said. "I have to be back to spell Mom by suppertime or soon after."

Edward pulled her so close she could feel his heartbeat beneath his shirt. "We can get a lot of alone time in before that. And I have to tell you, beautiful lady, I've sure been wanting some of that lately."

Mazie struggled to breathe, willing herself to keep a clear head, despite her desire to blurt out something like, "Let's just jump in the car and run off somewhere and get married!" Instead she held Edward's gaze with her own, returning his smile as she said, "I'll go check with Mom. Just give me a minute."

As she left him standing in the kitchen, she headed for her mother's room, where she could hear the muffled TV voices behind the closed door. She was relatively certain her mom was just resting and would be more than happy to stay with Mimi while she napped if it meant her only daughter could go out and spend some time with the man who so obviously loved her. Mazie just wished she knew if that relative certainty was a good thing ... or not.

CHAPTER FOURTEEN

On a scale of one to ten, the day was an eleven. Mazie couldn't deny it. Though Frisco was often socked in with fog, even during the afternoon hours, Langsdale was far enough inland that the sun was able to burn through the morning gray and wash the rolling countryside with golden warmth. As she sat beside Edward in his top-down convertible, cruising to whatever dreamy spot he had picked out, Mazie leaned her head back and sighed, enjoying the feel of the slightly cool breeze tossing her dark curls. Though she'd had some misgivings about breaking away to be alone with Edward, she was glad she'd done it. As much as she loved Mimi, she'd been spending far too much time cooped up in the house with her lately. Mazie could hardly wait for her teaching job to begin, though she knew that meant bringing in all-day caregivers for her great-grandmother.

Ninety-three, she thought. *Mimi seems so fragile at times, and yet I wonder what I'll be like at that age—if I even make it that far. I'm just glad she's still sharp mentally. I can't imagine not being able to talk with her or to listen to her stories.*

Thoughts of Harriet Tubman flooded her mind then, and she cut her eyes toward Edward. How was the story affecting him? Apart from some tense moments, he seemed to be enjoying it as much as she, but surely he had at least somewhat of a different take on it ... didn't he?

His jaw twitched as a smile curved the side of his lips, even as his eyes stayed focused on the road in front of him. "You're watching me," he said. "I can feel it."

"I sure can't get away with much, can I?"

"Nothing. Absolutely nothing. I told you before, I can feel it when you're watching me. Sometimes, I think I can even feel it when you're thinking about me."

She raised her eyebrows. "Is that right? And do you know what I'm thinking too?"

His smile faded only slightly. "I wish I could. At least, I think I wish that. Sometimes I'm not so sure."

Mazie dropped her eyes. She knew exactly what he meant, and with all her heart she wanted to ease his concerns. But since she wasn't completely clear on her own thoughts, how could she explain them to him? Most of the time she was certain she loved him. How could she not? But other times ... there was that something. What, she couldn't pinpoint, but more and more lately she wondered if it had something to do with her family.

Her ancestors, to be more exact. Both her mother and great-grandmother had always been so vague about their family history, particularly on her father's side. She scarcely remembered him and had experienced little or no contact with his part of the family either before or after he died. Was there something she should know about them? Would it change how she felt about herself ... or Edward?

"Your mind's going a mile a minute," Edward said. "I didn't mean to get you started on too much thinking. After all, we came out today to relax and enjoy ourselves, right?"

"Right." She smiled at him, even though he wasn't looking and made sure to insert an upbeat tone when she asked, "So where are we going anyway? You still haven't told me."

He took his eyes off the road long enough to wink at her. "You'll find out in a minute. We're almost there."

The look nearly melted her on the spot, and she couldn't help but think of how Harriet had been so taken by John Tubman's good looks and his charming ways. Had she done the right thing by marrying him, despite the fact he apparently didn't share her yearning for freedom?

Her wind-tossed curls settled down then, and she noticed Edward had slowed and put on his left-turn blinker. She frowned, studying the two-lane road that seemed to lead nowhere but into thicker stands of trees on both sides, nearly overshadowing them as they drove and blocking out the sun in places. This was not a destination she recognized, but she couldn't deny its charm as they withdrew farther from civilization and traffic and all the noise and commotion of everyday life. Whatever did her romantic Edward Clayton have in mind?

Within moments they were parked beside a meadow, encircled by whispering pines and sprinkled with brilliant wildflowers. When he turned off the engine, the only sound she heard was the distant caw of a crow.

"What do you think?" he said, turning toward her on the seat and stretching his arm across the back until it touched her shoulder. "Beautiful, isn't it?"

She nodded. "Incredibly so. I can't believe I've never been here before. How did you find it?"

"I didn't. Pops did." He turned and pointed off across the meadow, toward the right. "There's a little creek over there. Not much good for fishing, but full of pollywogs at the right time of year. Pops used to bring me down here and let me pull off my shoes and climb right into that icy cold creek. I'd take a jar with me and fill it full of water and as many pollywogs as I could catch. Mom hated it when I brought them home, but they never lived long anyway." He chuckled. "I'd always promise to catch flies and bugs to feed them, but that never worked out too well. I can't tell you how many jars of dead pollywogs I emptied out in the backyard. But Pops and I always had a great time out here, just the two of us."

Mazie smiled and nodded. "I can imagine. You really miss him, don't you?"

A temporary dampness touched his eyes. "Sure do. Probably always will. He was a great guy."

"I wish I could have known him."

"I do too. Though, as I'm sure you can imagine, he would have been surprised at our relationship. It wasn't exactly accepted in his day, you know."

Mazie hesitated before voicing a question she'd considered several times before. "Was he ... involved in the Civil Rights movement?"

"A little. Probably would have been more so if he'd lived in the South at the time, but the family had already moved out here long before that."

"Still," she said, "things must have been a lot different then. Did he ever talk to you about it?"

"Once in a while. I suppose he would have told me more if I'd shown much interest." He shrugged. "Guess I was just too focused on my own life issues to give much thought to his. Sometimes, I wonder just how much I've missed about my own heritage because of it." He dropped his eyes before looking back at her. "Mimi's stories about Harriett Tubman have really got me thinking about that."

She nodded. "I can imagine. And in a way, I know what you mean. There's a lot about my dad's family I don't know at all, and ... well, I wonder about it sometimes."

"Why don't you just ask your mom? I'm sure she'd tell you whatever you want to know."

"I have. And sure, she answers my questions—sort of. But she never gives me anything extra, if you know what I mean. Somehow I feel like ... oh, I don't know, like she's keeping something from me."

"Like what?"

"I have no idea. And I guess that's what bothers me most. Then again, it could be she really doesn't know any more than she's already told me."

His eyes flashed with insight before going back to soft, and she wanted to ask him what he had thought of in that moment, but she was afraid of the answer. Instead she smiled and said, "So, are we going to sit here in the car all day, or are you going to show me that creek full of pollywogs?"

Edward returned her smile. "Let's go. I even brought a couple of jars in the trunk. But if we end up with dead pollywogs in a few days, they're getting buried in your backyard."

Mazie laughed. "Deal," she said, and opened her door.

The feel of Mazie's hand in his as he drove toward her house early that evening was enough to sustain the hopeful emotions he'd experienced all afternoon. He could still hear her laughter and picture the sun glinting off her dark hair as they'd opted to leave the pollywogs where they were—if indeed there were any, as they hadn't really looked closely enough to find out. Mazie had dared to dip her toes into the icy creek but quickly withdrew them with a shriek. "It's freezing! I can't believe you actually got into that water!" They'd raced back to the car, laughing the entire way. Silently reviewing their day, Edward believed they'd connected in a way that included Mazie's letting her guard down—a rare occurrence, to say the least. And now he didn't want it to end.

He smiled as they drove into the setting sun, and he remembered the sound of their voices, singing silly children's songs together, songs he'd told her he'd learned from Pops. He'd been surprised to realize she knew a few of them and was willing to sing right along with him. For once, she hadn't been even slightly stiff or reserved, and he surely did like that side of her.

The breeze was getting cooler now, with the sun nearly gone for the day. When he sensed the edge of a shiver emanating from her shoulders, down her arm and right into the hand he held, he pulled over to put the top up on the car. While they waited for it to settle down above them, he leaned across the seat and closed his eyes, knowing she would respond. He longed to let his lips linger, but he also didn't want to do anything to break the sweet connection between them, so he pulled back after a brief kiss and smiled down at her before guiding the car back onto the road. When she reached up and placed her hand on his shoulder, gently kneading it as he drove, he wondered if it were possible to love anyone more than he loved Mazie Hartford.

And then he turned onto her street, and the connection he had so cherished was broken. Blinking red and white lights blanketed the street in front of Mazie's home, as the young woman beside him jerked upright in her seat.

"Oh," she cried. "Something's happened to Mimi!"

Edward had no doubt she was right. He could only pray they hadn't come back too late.

Mazie's heart raced nearly as fast as her feet as she tore from Edward's car, across the lawn, and up the porch steps toward the front door. She'd scarcely made it into the entryway when she spotted a gurney beside Mimi's bedroom door. A tall, hefty man wearing a "Langsdale Fire Department" T-shirt stood beside it, peering inside. Voices drifted out through the open door, alerting Mazie to the fact that others were inside with Mimi.

She slowed her pace only slightly until she reached the gurney. The fireman turned his attention from what was going on inside the room toward the new arrival. He raised his eyebrows questioningly.

"Family," she said. "I live here."

He nodded and stepped back just enough to allow her the space she needed to catch a glimpse of another fireman and two paramedics gathered around Mimi's bed, poking and prodding and questioning. Mazie's mother was also in the room, answering their inquiries and supplying the required medical information.

Lilly glanced up and caught Mazie's eyes. Her chin trembled as she smiled, and Mazie knew her mother was doing what she could to reassure her all was under control, but Mazie could also tell her mother was deeply concerned.

"What happened?" Mazie mouthed, but before Lilly could answer, the paramedics were lifting Mimi between them, gently transferring her to the gurney in the hallway.

Mazie stepped back to give them room, but not before she saw the ashen look on her beloved great-grandmother's face. Her heart constricted at the sight, even as she retreated further down the hallway to allow the paramedics to wheel

Mimi toward the front door. She'd hoped to hear the elderly woman speak a word of encouragement, but her thin lips were pressed together and her eyes closed tight. An oxygen tube had already been fitted into her nostrils.

Once they'd passed her and reached the front door, Mazie tore her gaze away and looked back toward Mimi's room. Her mother stood in the doorway, her face nearly as pale as Mimi's. Mazie rushed to her and fell into her embrace.

"Is she going to be okay?" she gasped, swallowing a sob. "What happened, Mom?"

She felt her mother shrug. "I don't really know," she said, stroking Mazie's hair. "I had tucked her in for the night, and though she seemed exceptionally tired, I didn't think much about it. It's been a long day for her, after all. But ..." Her voice trailed off, and Mazie heard her sigh. "I was about to go to bed myself when I felt like I should check on her one more time. When I did ..." Another pause, and a shake of her head. "She looked terrible. So pale and ... lifeless. When I leaned down and placed my cheek by her lips, I realized she was barely breathing. That's when I called 911."

Mazie shivered at the thought. They all knew Mimi was nearing the end of her life and could go at any time, but that didn't mean they would welcome her leaving. It was nearly impossible to imagine their life without the opinionated but kind-hearted woman.

"Will she ... be all right now?" Mazie asked, pulling back to look into her mother's eyes.

Lilly paused. "I hope so," she whispered. "We just need to pray."

Mazie nodded, suddenly aware they were no longer alone in the hallway. She glanced up to find Edward standing beside them. When their eyes connected, he opened his arms and encircled them both. "Let's pray right now," he said. "Then we'll get in my car, and I'll drive you to the hospital."

CHAPTER FIFTEEN

The three of them huddled on adjoining plastic chairs in the waiting room, having completed the necessary paperwork right after they arrived. Mimi had been whisked into an emergency room cubicle, where the on-call doctor immediately began a thorough examination, asking Mazie and the others to wait outside until he was done.

"It's been a long time," Mazie said, speaking in hushed tones among the other individuals and families who occupied the busy room, many waiting for hours to see a physician. "Shouldn't they have called us in by now?"

Edward's arm lay across her shoulders, and he squeezed her reassuringly. She leaned against him, grateful for his strength and concern, but her eyes were fixed on her mother.

Tears sparkled in Lilly's dark eyes, but she blinked them away. "I'm sure they'll call us any moment now," she said, but Mazie sensed she was offering reassurance she didn't necessarily feel herself. "Besides, I called Mimi's regular doctor, and he's on the way. Once he gets here, we should know more."

Mazie nodded, realizing there was no sense pushing the issue because her mother simply didn't have any more information to offer. There really wasn't anything they could do now but continue to wait ... and pray.

Her heart warmed at the memory of the brief but heartfelt prayer Edward had offered before they left to follow the ambulance to the hospital. How grateful and blessed she was to have such a strong believer by her side! Surely he was the sort of husband every Christian woman dreams of finding one day, and here he was, sitting next to her, ready to slip a ring on her finger if she would only say yes.

I can't think about that now. Tonight is about Mimi—not me or my fickle feelings. Oh, Lord, please let her be all right! Please don't take her from us yet, Father.

The thought occurred to her then that her mother really should have called her while awaiting the ambulance for Mimi. Why hadn't she? She felt her eyes widen and her heart sink as she remembered she had turned off her cell phone when she and Edward got out of the car to explore the creek and surrounding countryside that afternoon. No doubt she'd neglected to turn it back on.

A quick rummage in her purse and glance at the phone confirmed her suspicion as guilt flooded through her. She'd known Mimi wasn't feeling well this afternoon. Why had she allowed herself to get so caught up in her own little world that she'd neglected to make herself available to others who might need her?

Stop it. You're being silly. It's not like you left her alone. Mom was there, and she did the only thing anyone could do in the situation. Do you really think you could have done any better?

As if reading her thoughts, Edward feathered a light kiss on top of her head, and she relaxed slightly, though she knew she wouldn't get past her anxiety completely until someone came out from the cubicle where Mimi lay and filled them in on her condition. She just wanted to be told her great-grandmother was all right, and they could go back and see her, touch her, speak with her.

A door opened then—not the one she'd hoped for, with a doctor or nurse coming out with news—but the outside door. Tracy stepped through it, glanced around the crowded room, and then moved in their direction the moment she spotted their group against the wall.

"How is she?" she asked as she drew up even with them. "Any word?"

Mazie raised her eyebrows. How had she known? Silly question. Edward no doubt called her. Did he ever miss a beat?

He got up and offered his chair to his sister, but she shook her head. "I'm fine. Really. I just wanted to see how she's doing and if there's anything I can do to help."

Lilly smiled up at her. "Just pray," she said, "and know we so appreciate your support."

Tracy nodded. "Absolutely. So do you know anything yet? I thought at least one of you would be back there with her by now."

"Hopefully soon," Lilly said. "The emergency room doctor is with her now, and we're waiting for Mimi's personal physician to arrive."

A whoosh interrupted their conversation, and they all turned toward the now-open door that led back to the cubicles. A man in a white coat, with a stethoscope around his neck, peered around the room. Mazie recognized him immediately as the doctor who had told them to wait while he examined Mimi.

Lilly and Mazie jumped to their feet beside Tracy and Edward as the doctor spotted them and stepped in their direction. Mazie felt Edward's arm slip around her waist, and once again she was overwhelmed with gratitude for his strength and support as she waited for what she prayed was good news about the elderly women who meant so very much to her.

Congestive heart failure. COPD. The words echoed in Mazie's heart and mind. The doctor had explained the conditions were certainly not unusual in someone Mimi's age—in fact, they were quite common—but he hadn't been able to give them the assurance Mazie had hoped for, the words that would tell her Mimi was going to be fine and would continue to be with them for quite a while to come.

Maybe when her regular doctor gets here. She was reluctant to voice her concerns to the others, as she knew they too were processing the diagnosis and its implications. "She's resting comfortably," the doctor had said, just before announcing he had recommended she be moved to a room and kept for observation over the next couple of days. Would Mimi's doctor concur? Would he give them more information and, most important, greater hope for Mimi's recovery?

She's ninety-three, Mazie reminded herself, as she awaited her turn to visit her great-grandmother. Lilly had gone in first, promising to be back in five minutes, so Mazie now sat between Edward and Tracy. Her stomach churned at the thought of what she would find when she went through those double doors and back to the cubicle where Mimi lay. Was she awake now? Would she recognize her? Would they be able to have a conversation?

The doors whooshed open again, and this time it was her mother who stepped through them. She was smiling, but Mazie recognized the positive expression was stilted and forced. She sighed as Lilly approached. It was her turn to visit Mimi.

"How is she?" she asked, willing her mother to give an encouraging report.

Lilly's smile was even tighter than Mazie had realized. "She's ... as well as can be expected for now. Like the doctor said, she's resting comfortably. She's on oxygen and IV's, and lots of monitors, so don't be alarmed when you see all that. They're going to get her to a room as soon as possible, and Dr. Marsh should be here any moment."

Mazie nodded. She wished she could have gone in with her mother, but the doctor had explained patients in emergency could have only one visitor at a time. That ruled out Edward's accompanying her as well, and the thought left her legs wobbly.

"I'll ... I'll go in now," she said.

Edward took her hand and squeezed, a gesture she quickly returned before releasing his grip and stepping toward the double doors. How was it her great-grandmother had earned such a huge place in her heart in such a short time? The only times they'd ever really spent together were the summer in hot, humid Prattville, Alabama, and the few years Mimi had been with them in the Bay Area. Yet Mazie knew her great-grandmother's imminent departure would leave a huge void in her life.

Taking a deep breath, she passed through the doors and on into the entryway on the other side where cloth curtains separated patients and offered a bit of privacy.

Third cubicle on the right, she reminded herself.

The curtain was drawn, and Mazie spotted her great-grandmother the moment she stepped past cubicle number two. Though Mimi's color was slightly better than when the paramedics had wheeled her from their home earlier that evening, she was still pale, her cheeks sunken and her eyes shut tight. Monitors beeped and numbers blinked from screens. The smell of antiseptic irritated her already-churning stomach. Should she try to speak to Mimi? Would she even hear her if she did?

Mazie decided she had to try. Even if Mimi didn't respond, perhaps she would hear her and know she was there.

"Mimi?" The word came out as more of a croak than an actual voice, and Mazie could only pray Mimi had heard and understood.

"Mimi, it's me, Mazie."

She waited, but when Mimi showed no signs of movement, she tried again.

"I just wanted you to know I'm here," she said, leaning down to speak close to Mimi's ear. "So are Mom and Edward. Tracy too. We're all here, praying for you and waiting for Dr. Marsh to arrive."

Hot tears suddenly stung her eyes, but no matter how hard she tried to blink them away, they continued to come, overflowing from her eyelids onto her cheeks. "Oh, Mimi," she whispered. "Don't leave us. Not yet! We love you. We need you here with us."

Mimi still didn't move, and Mazie sank down on a metal folding chair beside the bed, taking her great-grandmother's hand in hers and caressing the paper-thin skin with her thumb. "We want you to come back home with us, Mimi. Please get better. Please, Mimi."

She spotted a small box of tissues on the bedside stand and snagged one with her spare hand. Mopping her face, she was suddenly aware of how short five minutes could be—and how very fragile life itself was when all else was stripped away and eternity hung in the balance.

Midnight was nearly upon them by the time Edward dropped Lilly and Mazie off at home. He hadn't stayed but had instead followed Tracy in her car to make sure she got home all right. Lilly noticed Mazie hadn't even tried to convince him to come inside, and she imagined it was because each of them was as exhausted as the other. They'd done all they could do for the time being. Now they all needed some rest.

Thank goodness I have tomorrow off, Lilly thought, putting the kettle on to boil for a quick cup of tea before turning in. Though she was tired, she knew she needed to unwind a bit before hitting the bed, or she'd just find herself getting a second wind and staring into the darkness for the next couple of hours. The shop wasn't closed on Mondays, as many were, but Lilly usually opted to give the day's clients to her coworker and reserve the day to herself except for rare occasions.

"Fixing tea?"

Mazie's voice behind her interrupted her thoughts, and she turned to see her daughter standing in the kitchen doorway. Lilly nodded. "Want to join me?"

Mazie shrugged. "Sure. Why not? I probably can't sleep yet anyway."

In moments, they were seated across from one another at the kitchen table, a steaming mug of chamomile in front of each of them. Lilly had offered Mazie a cookie, but she'd declined. Lilly wasn't in the mood for one either.

"She's going to be all right, you know," Lilly offered.

Mazie raised her eyes from her tea and blinked at Lilly. "Do you really think so?"

Lilly smiled. "I know so." She swallowed before continuing. "Now, I don't know that she'll recover and come back here and everything will be as it was, but I do know she'll be okay no matter what happens. Your great-grandmother has a strong faith, and she knows without question where she will go when she takes her last breath on earth. You know that too, right? She's in God's hands, Mazie, whatever happens."

"I know that," she said, her voice a cracking whisper. "That doesn't mean it's easy to think we might lose her."

Lilly nodded. "Of course not. It's never easy to say goodbye to someone we love, even temporarily. But we really need to stay focused on that great truth, Mazie. The Bible says when someone we love dies, we grieve, but not as those who have no hope. We know we'll see Mimi again because we know she rests in the Father's hands, whether in this life or the next."

Lilly saw the flicker of pain in her daughter's eyes. "I'll miss her," she said simply.

"As will I," Lilly said, "whenever that time comes." She reached across the table and laid her hand on Mazie's. "Even if she gets better and comes home this time, you know it can't be long. Sweetheart, she's ninety-three years old."

Tears spilled again from Mazie's dark eyes, and she nodded. "I know," she said in a voice so small Lilly remembered how her child had sounded years ago. She knew too Mazie was thinking of the story Mimi was telling her about the Moses quilt. Would the frail old woman live long enough to finish the story? And if she didn't, what then? Lilly had always sensed there was something special about the quilt and its story, possibly even something that would unlock a secret in their very own family, and yet

Mimi had never shared it with her. If Lilly's grandmother died, the story might very well die with her, and somehow Lilly sensed that would be a very great tragedy.

But this was no time to voice those concerns to Mazie. They would simply have to continue to pray for God's perfect will in the situation and then trust Him for the outcome.

CHAPTER SIXTEEN

Mimi felt as if she were floating. In and out, back and forth, up and down—and yet never moving from the same spot. Where was she? Nothing was familiar. This certainly wasn't her room back in the old house in Prattville, and it wasn't her room at Lilly's either. What was going on? How had she come to this strange place?

Beep, beep, beep. The noise was constant and just loud enough to annoy her. Muted voices teased her ears, but they were too far away to distinguish the words. Where were Lilly and Mazie? Why didn't they come to explain things to her?

She tried to open her eyes. They felt heavy, but she managed. A monitor of some sort seemed to pulse with light and jagged shapes, almost in time with the beeping. She lifted her eyes and saw a metal pole with a bag of clear liquid hanging from it. A tube snaked downward. She followed it to the spot where it was attached to the back of her hand.

A needle. Why do I have a needle taped to my hand?

She lifted her free hand and fumbled with another plastic tube on her face, pulling it free from her nose. In moments, a pudgy-faced woman, dressed in white, appeared beside her, gazing down with a warm smile.

"Well, now," she said, "so you're awake. And getting into mischief already, I see." She retrieved the plastic tube and replaced the two small protrusions in her nostrils. Mimi realized then she was receiving oxygen.

"Am I ..." She struggled to speak, her mouth and throat dry. "Hospital?"

The smiling lady in white, obviously a nurse, nodded. "Yes, ma'am, you are. And I'm glad to see you're doing better. Your family will certainly be relieved too."

My family. So Lilly and Mazie were there too—or at least had been at some point. She felt a fraction of relief at the thought. "Where ... are they ... now?"

"We sent them home to get some rest." The nurse, whose nametag Mimi had now spotted and deciphered that it read Sharon, patted Mimi's hand. "It was getting late, and we finally convinced them we could take care of you just fine. They promised to come back first thing in the morning."

Mimi could scarcely smile, but she did her best, letting her heavy eyelids close again. Now she had something to look forward to—her family coming. And she was determined to convince them to take her home immediately. She certainly didn't need to be in the hospital. There was nothing wrong with her but a little old age, and even the doctors and nurses couldn't cure that. She was running out of steam and time, and the truth of that fact didn't concern her one bit. Her only concern was getting back home so she could finish telling Mazie and Edward the story about the Moses quilt. The old woman sensed it might be her last assignment on earth, and she didn't want to fail in completing it. Besides, she also sensed that Mazie and Edward's future together just might hang in the balance.

Two days passed, with Mimi regaining a tiny bit of strength and quite a bit of feistiness. They'd managed to avoid direct answers to her demands to come home immediately, but Mazie knew they wouldn't be able to put her off much longer.

"What do you think, Dr. Marsh?" Lilly asked, as she and Mazie stood outside Mimi's door after the doctor finished examining his patient. "Is she well enough to come home?"

The middle-aged physician with the graying hair and prematurely lined face raised his eyebrows. "That's always iffy," he said. "I can't give you any guarantees. She does seem quite a bit better than when she came in a few days ago, but at her age and with her health conditions, she could regress at any time. Still, if you two can work out your schedules so one of you is always with her—either you or a professional caregiver—then I don't see any reason I can't release her this afternoon. I'm sure she'd be much happier at home with the two of you."

"You can say that again," came a surprisingly strong retort from Mimi's room.

The two women and the doctor could scarcely swallow their laughter. "She's hard of hearing," Lilly whispered, "but she can hear what she wants to hear."

Dr. Marsh nodded, still smiling. "I have several patients who fit that description." He jotted something on a chart and looked up. "All right. I'm going to order her release. It'll take a couple of hours to get everything processed, but if you don't mind hanging around awhile, you should be able to have her home before suppertime."

"Speaking of which," Lilly said, "what can she eat?"

"Stick with liquids for now," he said. "Clear soups, gelatin, apple juice. That sort of thing. And of course, those nutritional drinks are very good. If she starts complaining she's hungry and wants something more, just give me a call, and we'll see if we can ease her onto something a little more solid."

Leaving her mother and the doctor to finalize details, Mazie slipped back into Mimi's room. Her heart swelled to see her awake, leaning on her pillow in her propped-up bed. Her gray hair was askew, and she was still connected to wires and machines, but Mazie thought she'd never looked more beautiful.

"Hi, Mimi," she said, smiling as she sat down next to her great-grandmother's bed. "How are you feeling?"

"Good enough to get out of this place," she groused. "Did I hear right? Is that doctor of mine finally going to let me out of here?"

Mazie nodded. "He's going to start the paperwork now, but he said it'll take a couple of hours."

"Humph. How much paperwork does it take to sign me out? I never heard of such ... nonsense."

Mazie saw the weariness seep back into Mimi's eyes, and she knew the extended conversation was taking its toll. She laid a hand on Mimi's arm. "Just relax, Mimi. You don't want to get all worked up and then have them say you aren't well enough to go home after all, do you? You need to rest and relax and just be a little patient. We'll have you back in your own room before you know it."

Mimi eyed her for a moment, as if weighing her words, before nodding and closing her eyes. "I suppose you're right, child. Of course you are. I'll rest now. You just promise to wake me as soon as you're ready to roll me out of here."

"I promise. And believe me, I'm looking forward to it almost as much as you are." She knew the majority of "Mimi-sitting" would fall on her shoulders, since her mom had already taken off quite a bit of time from work over the last few days and couldn't afford much more. But Mazie didn't mind. Seeing Mimi carried out of the house on a gurney had brought the reality of the woman's impending death into sharper focus, and Mazie was determined to enjoy every minute she could with her great-grandmother— before it was too late.

As Mazie had hoped, her great-grandmother thrived once she was back in familiar territory. Within a couple of days, she had graduated from liquids to a soft diet, though she still complained about it and wanted to know when she could have some pizza or chop suey and eggrolls. Lilly and Mazie humored her as best they could, sticking to the doctor's dietary suggestions and coaxing Mimi to accept them as what was best for her.

"Humph," she said more than once. "How does a doctor who hasn't even reached fifty yet know what's best for me? Does he think he can keep me here forever, eating pudding and applesauce? I'd rather have one good day of steak and baked potatoes than five years of mush."

"I know, Mimi," Mazie soothed. "But you have to think about us. We love you and would miss you terribly if you left us."

Mimi squinted one eye before answering. "Well, you might as well accept that I'm getting out of here ahead of you, no matter what you feed me."

Mazie's heart squeezed at the truth of it, but she smiled and urged Mimi to have another bite of oatmeal. "Humph," the old woman said, but she ate it anyway.

By the time ten days had rolled around since her ambulance trip to the hospital, Mimi was very nearly back to her old self, though she didn't sit in her wheelchair nearly as long at a stretch. Mazie couldn't help but notice how much more time her great-grandmother spent in bed, sleeping, but at least she was home with them where she belonged.

As Mazie tucked her into bed that night, Mimi laid a frail hand on her arm. "I miss Edward," she said. "Why not invite him over tomorrow, and we can get back to our story?"

Mazie raised her eyebrows. "Are you sure, Mimi? Do you really feel up to it?"

"Of course I do," she insisted. "You get him over here, and I'll give you the next installment of the Moses quilt story."

"You do know he has to work tomorrow, right?"

"Then tell him to come over when he's done." She winked and grinned, her lips caving in because Mazie had already put Mimi's teeth in the container to soak for the night. "You might suggest he bring me something good to eat while he's at it."

"Oh now, Mimi, you know Edward's not going to go against the doctor's orders." She grinned. "But if I ask him real nice, maybe he'll bring some of your favorite raspberry sherbet from the market down the street."

Mimi's eyes lit up and her smile broadened. "Now that's the best idea I've heard in a while." She nodded. "Yes, you tell that handsome young man to come over with raspberry sherbet tomorrow, and I'll give you both another installment on the story. We've got quite a way to go to finish it, and since I don't know how much longer I'll be hanging around this place, we'd better get to work."

CHAPTER SEVENTEEN

"Are you sure she's up to it?"

Edward's dark eyes reflected his sincere concern, and Mazie's heart warmed at his tenderness. She smiled as they stood face-to-face in the entryway, her hands on his chest as she gazed up at him.

"She insists she is," Mazie answered. "In fact, it was her idea. She's insistent we get back to the story." She allowed her smile to fade as she fought the tears she knew were visible to Edward. "She ..." Mazie swallowed. "She said she wants to finish it before it's too late."

Edward's smile was soft as he pulled her close. "Then we need to honor her wishes," he whispered, his chin resting on the top of her head. "This is important to her, Mazie. And for whatever reason, she apparently believes it's important to us too."

Mazie knew he was right, though she couldn't quite grasp the reason for Mimi's urgency. Perhaps part of her wasn't ready to acknowledge the reason.

Shaking off the thought, she pulled back and said, "Let's go then. She's in bed, waiting for us."

"Is your mom going to join us?"

"No. She's taken so much time off lately while Mimi's been in the hospital that she has to make up for it by working a few evenings for a while."

Edward turned toward Mimi's room, placed his hand under Mazie's elbow, and escorted her down the hallway. "How did she do today? Is she still eating better?"

"Pretty good, actually. She's graduated from soup and pudding and seems very glad of it. Today she ate an entire tuna sandwich, probably the most I've seen her eat at one time since all this happened."

Edward smiled down at her as they reached Mimi's doorway, where muted TV voices drifted out to them. "I'm glad to hear it—not only for Mimi's sake but for yours too. I know how hard this has been on you."

Tears stung her eyes again, and she nodded. "I love her so much," she whispered. "I just can't imagine what it will be like when she's ... gone."

Edward brushed a tear from her cheek, tilted her chin upward, and kissed her forehead. "Well, she's not gone yet, so let's enjoy every minute we have with her until then."

Mazie nodded and opened the door, peering in to be sure her great-grandmother was still awake. "Mimi?"

The old woman lay propped up against her pillows, just as Mazie had left her. Without even opening her eyes, she motioned with her hand for them to come in. "Turn off the television, will you, dear?" she said. "I'm not paying any attention to it anyway."

Mazie smiled. Mimi nearly always had the TV on, but unless it was one of her favorite shows, she usually made the point she wasn't really watching or listening. Mazie retrieved the remote from the bed stand and hit the power button before sitting down in one of two chairs beside Mimi's bed. Edward quickly lowered himself into the other.

Mimi turned her head toward them and opened her eyes, a smile spreading across her face at the sight of Edward. "I've missed you," she said, her rheumy eyes twinkling as he took her hand.

"I've missed you too," he said. "I'm so glad to see you looking better."

Mimi's chuckle was weak and nearly morphed into a cough, but she recovered before it did. "If this is looking better," she quipped, "I must have really looked terrible before."

Edward raised her hand to his lips and kissed it. "You did give us quite a scare, you know."

She nodded. "I realize that. But you realize too that I'm ninety-three years old, right? I can't hang around here forever." She winked at him. "To tell you the truth, I wouldn't want to. I have better things to do, after all."

Mazie's chest hurt as she watched two of the three people in her life who were most dear to her interacting with one another as if they were already family. Would they ever be—truly? Would Mazie finally get past her doubts and misgivings enough to marry this wonderful man before Mimi moved on? Mazie realized at that moment how sad it would be to walk down the aisle and become Edward's wife without Mimi there to celebrate the occasion.

Then again, that's hardly a reason to get married, she thought, pulling herself together and clearing her throat. "Well," she said, "now that we're back in our usual spots, should I get the quilt? Are you ready to give us the next installment of your story?"

Mimi turned her attention from Edward to Mazie. "I certainly am," she said, pointing. "Yes, please, get the quilt. I believe I saw it sitting on top of the chest over there."

Mazie retrieved the patchwork piece and held it up for Mimi to see. "Which part will we be hearing about tonight?"

"We'll pick up where we left off," Mimi said, "after Harriet's marriage to John, when her passion to be free still burned strong in her heart, she quickly realized her new husband didn't share her desires." She shook her head, her eyes going dim. "That was a hard realization for Harriet, who had dreamed she and John would escape together and start a life away from slave territory, once and for all."

"But it didn't work that way?" Mazie questioned.

"I'm afraid not. You see that patch with what looks like bars and a bird on it?"

Mazie and Edward focused on the quilt. When they both nodded and asserted they did indeed see it, Mimi said, "That's the patch that represents Harriet's courageous decision to be free, regardless of the cost. Like a bird being let out of a cage, our heroine was just about ready to fly."

Harriet couldn't sleep. Lying next to John, feeling his warmth and listening to his steady breathing, she reminded herself how blessed she was to have such a good and kind man for a husband. And yet ... he wasn't willing to even discuss her plans or dreams for freedom. The man was perfectly content to live out his life in this dirt-floored, one-room shack, working for the master, living on scraps, and being grateful for his free status that, for the most part, guaranteed no one beat or abused him.

Harriet did not share her husband's contentment. For one thing, she hadn't had an abuse-free life. She'd been beaten, whipped, starved, and humiliated more times than she could remember, and her desire for freedom grew with every abuse. Not only did Harriet long to be free herself, but she also wanted to help free as many of her people as possible. Why couldn't John understand that?

Harriet glanced over at him in the semidarkness, the faint light of the moon shining through their one high, unpaned window. John Tubman was a handsome man, and a charming one too. And oh, could he sing! He was quite a catch, that one. That he'd even noticed Harriet was no small miracle in her way of thinking. But it wasn't enough. She'd tried to convince herself it was, but her attempts had fallen short.

It's because he's free. Don't nobody own him like they do me.

This thought had rolled through Harriet's mind many times during her brief marriage. John was just a boy when he and his family were freed at the time of their master's death—as stipulated in the man's will. But free or not, there wasn't much opportunity for Blacks to make a living except as farmers or field hands, working right alongside the slaves. As a result, free Blacks and slaves often married as in John and Harriet's case. And though John remained free after the wedding ceremony, Harriet was still a slave. If they were to live together, they would do so in the slaves' quarters. The only difference was John always kept his papers on him, ready to produce them and prove his free status whenever needed.

To make matters worse, Harriet had come to believe she and her family had been set free as well, but she had no way to prove it. Her mother had told her about an arrangement made with her former master when she was still young. According to the terms, Harriet's mother would serve her master's granddaughter and the granddaughter's children until the granddaughter died or Harriet's mother turned forty-five, whichever came first. At one point, Harriet managed to pay a lawyer five dollars to find proof of this arrangement. The lawyer did, and Harriet learned her mother should have been set free years earlier, but a deceptive master refused to honor the agreement. As a result, Harriet's mother and the entire family remained in slavery. Without funds to hire a lawyer to pursue the matter, there was nothing to be done about it.

Watching her beloved John sleep, she wondered at the difference. Was there any ... really? Her husband was legally free, and yet he lived much like any of the slaves on the plantation. In Harriet's mind, that wasn't free—at least not the sort of freedom she wanted.

But though the thoughts and questions of that night continued to roll through Harriet's heart and mind, she stayed at her husband's side. They had no children, but she loved John deeply and took great comfort in their relationship—until 1849, when everything changed.

Harriet's master, the young heir to the Brodas Plantation, died suddenly, and rumors began to fly. To shore up some of the economic losses incurred over the years, the guardian of the estate planned to sell off several slaves. Harriet and two of her brothers were among them. They would be sent from Maryland, where John and the rest of her family would stay, to Georgia, where she would most likely be sold on the auction block. The possibilities horrified her, particularly being separated from her loved ones—most likely never to see them again. Harriet was not willing to accept that fate without a fight.

The North called to her, a place where she could be free. Surely John would agree to come with her now ... wouldn't he? And when they were settled, she would come back for her parents and siblings. At least, that was her plan. Now all she had to do was convince John to join her.

Edward's hand on her arm pulled Mazie back from that time in 1849, when Harriet discovered she was about to be sold to a slave owner in Georgia. The implications were staggering. No wonder the courageous young woman determined to escape at last! How could her husband do anything but agree with her?

She glanced down at Edward's hand before shifting her eyes upward into his—but not before noting the contrast of his dark skin against hers. What must it be like to know your ancestors were more than likely slaves? Though Edward had told her long ago he had no idea if that were true, he'd also said he imagined it was. What was he thinking now, as he listened to Mimi's stories of Harriet Tubman and her longing to be free? Having been raised in an upper-middle-class family without experiencing any serious hardships of any kind, could he honestly relate at all?

Edward leaned close and whispered, "I think she's asleep."

Mazie blinked in surprise. She'd been so caught up in the story she hadn't noticed when Mimi drifted off. Turning to look at her great-grandmother, she realized Edward was right. Her eyes were closed and her breathing was even. Mimi was finished for the night.

Mazie stood and pulled the covers up under Mimi's chin and then folded the quilt and laid it back on the chest before following Edward out the door and down the hallway toward the kitchen. She crossed immediately to the stove and picked up the kettle.

"How about some tea?" she asked, her back to Edward as she filled the kettle with water. "I'm going to have some."

She felt him step up behind her and slide his arms around her waist. His lips were very near the back of her neck as he talked, sending a delicious shiver down her spine. "If it means I can stay here with you longer, I'll drink as many cups of tea as you can make."

Placing the full kettle back on the stove and flipping on the burner, she turned in Edward's arms and leaned in against his chest, listening to the steady pounding of his heart. She felt so safe here, so ... at home. What possible reason could she have for resisting a lifetime of such love and devotion?

She sighed. Perhaps, if Mimi was able to continue her story to the end, Mazie might find the answer to her dilemma. At least, she certainly hoped so.

CHAPTER EIGHTEEN

Lilly's feet hurt, and she couldn't wait to finish her last comb out and head for home. The stress of worrying about Mimi and now trying to make up for lost time—and money— after taking off work for a few days were taking their toll. Lilly was especially concerned with Mazie's reaction when Mimi finally passed on, which was bound to be sooner rather than later.

She applied a touch of spray to the elderly woman's bluish curls and handed her a mirror so she could check her new look from all sides. *Not that it's very new. Shirley hasn't let me change her hair in twenty years. Same color, same length, same curls. But it makes her happy, so I guess that's what counts.*

"I think it needs a bit more hairspray," Shirley commented, touching the top of her hair. "I don't want it to blow in the wind."

Lilly smiled. With the amount of hairspray Shirley insisted on using, her hair wouldn't move in a tornado. But she accommodated her and lacquered her hair to sustain any storm that might come her way.

Shirley wrote out her check, slowly and painstakingly, including her usual three-dollar tip, and waved goodbye before heading out the door. The bell tinkled behind her, and Lilly sighed with relief. Her day was done. A quick ten-minute cleanup plus locking up her funds in the safe, and she'd be on her way.

I wonder if Mimi shared any more of her Harriet Tubman story with Mazie and Edward. She said she was planning to, but I can't help but wonder how much longer she'll be able to continue doing that. With her heart and lungs failing, storytelling must be a real drain for her.

She swept up the last of the hair strands from the floor and deposited them in the trash can, picturing how frail her grandmother had appeared as she lay against the white sheets and pillowcases that morning before Lilly left for work. She'd known for some time that Mimi's days on earth were drawing to a close, but now she could see it. It was as if the dear woman was fading away, right before their eyes. Did Mazie see it too? Surely she did.

Lilly opened the wall safe and tucked the day's profits inside. She was grateful for Edward. He was the strength and stability Mazie needed. Why couldn't the girl see that? Perhaps she did, and still she hesitated.

All was finished now, and Lilly grabbed her purse and jacket and headed for the front door. It would be good to get home and kick off her shoes at last. Maybe she'd even treat herself to a nice long soak in the tub before heading for bed.

Edward watched Mazie as she stirred her tea. She'd been at it for a while now, and the sugar was no doubt dissolved. Quite obviously her mind was somewhere else.

"Hey there, beautiful," he said, laying his hand on hers and effectively stopping her mindless stirring. "What are you thinking about?"

Mazie's head jerked slightly, as she lifted her eyes to meet his. He saw the questions swirling there and longed to offer answers, but something told him he didn't have any to offer.

"Sorry," she mumbled, a weak smile accompanying the one-word apology. "Guess I'm still thinking about Mimi's story."

He nodded. "Me too. I can't imagine what it was like for Harriet, learning she and her brothers were about to go on the auction block and not sure if the man she loved would be willing to escape with her or not. I mean, seriously, how could he do otherwise? To ask her to stay would be tantamount to agreeing to let her be sold off and the two of them being separated forever." He increased the pressure of his hand on hers. "I can't imagine letting anything come between us, baby. No matter how big a mountain that tried to separate us, I'd find a way to move it."

Tears pooled in her eyes, and she nodded. "I know you would," she whispered. "And I love you for that."

His heart soared. It wasn't that she'd never declared her love for him, but she didn't do so often, and certainly not lightly. When she said it, she meant it, and he received it as the gift it was. If only he could be sure her love would one day extend to a lifetime commitment, but so far, she'd refused to take that final step. And so he continued to wait, hoping and praying he wasn't just wasting his time.

"So," he said at last, "what do you think? Is Mimi just telling us the great story behind her special Moses quilt, or is she heading somewhere with it? Somehow I get the feeling there's more to it, don't you?"

Mazie nodded. "I do, yes. She seems so adamant about finishing it, even though I know it's difficult for her, especially now with her ... weak heart and all."

Her words trailed off at the end, and Edward squeezed her hand again. How would Mazie take it when Mimi died? For surely it couldn't be much longer now. He hoped she would let him stay close enough throughout the ordeal to be the strength he knew she would need to get through it. *And, you'd better stay close to the One who gives you strength in the first place—or you won't have any to offer Mazie.*

Tracy hadn't yet turned in for the night when her cell phone rang. She flipped it open and looked at the screen.

Edward. Unusual for him to call at this hour. I wonder what's up.

"Hey, big brother," she said after punching the receive button. "What are you doing calling your baby sister at this hour? I thought you'd still be hanging out with your sweetheart."

"I was. Went over there after work and then spent some time listening to more of her great-grandmother's stories about Harriet Tubman."

She raised her eyebrows. "We studied about old Moses when we were in school, right? She was a great lady, no doubt about it. But what's the fascination now?"

After a slight hesitation, he said, "It's just ... personal somehow. I can't really explain it, but Mimi's story, told against the background of her Moses quilt, brings it all to life I guess."

Tracy could almost see him shrug, and she smiled as she pictured his little-boy look. "Okay, so the story is personal now. Is that what you called to tell me?"

"Not really. We had a quick bite to eat when I first got there, but I'm kind of hungry now. Are you and the folks in bed yet?"

"Mom and Dad are, and I was just about to head that way. Why?"

"If you're still dressed, I'll take you out for pie. What do you think?"

Tracy grinned. "I think you know how to get to me, Bro. What kind of pie and where?"

"Your choice on both."

"It's a date. Give me a few minutes."

"I'll be there in fifteen."

She glanced at her watch. "I'll be ready," she said, and then flipped the phone shut and hurried to her room to touch up her makeup and change into something a bit more presentable. Her date might just be her brother, but you never knew who you might run into when you were out and about.

She was running a pick through her hair when she heard Edward let himself in the front door. With one last glance in the mirror, she flipped off her bedroom light and hurried out to meet him.

CHAPTER NINETEEN

The restaurant was nearly empty by the time Edward and Tracy slid into a booth and began to browse the dessert menu. Generic pop tunes from the '80s and '90s played in the background.

"Not very busy tonight," Edward commented, peering at his sister over the top of his menu.

"It's ten o'clock on Wednesday," Tracy said without looking up. "What did you expect?"

"I expected you to pick a popular place, somewhere with a reputation for the best pies in the entire world."

She laughed, this time flicking her eyes up at him before looking back at the menu. "In Langsdale? Seriously? If it weren't so late, we could head into Frisco and find a hot spot there, but we do have to work tomorrow, you know."

It was Edward's turn to laugh. "You're not getting old and fuddy-duddy on me, are you? The Tracy I know could stay up all night and still make it to work in the morning without missing a beat."

"Yeah, well, I can still do that with the right incentive. No offense, but it takes more than a piece of pie with my favorite big brother."

Edward feigned offense. "You really know how to hurt a guy, don't you?"

She looked up and offered an exaggerated sigh. "So are you going to order some pie or not?"

He returned to his menu. "Fine. Pie it is. Coconut cream looks good."

"Not to me. I want lots of fruit in mine, warmed up and smothered in vanilla ice cream."

Edward shook his head. "You'd better be glad you've got a good metabolism, Sis. The way you eat, you'd be as big as a house if you didn't."

She swished her menu at him. "And what about you? Mama always said you'd eat anything that didn't eat you first."

"Hey, that's when I was a kid. I'm a grown-up now, and I'll have you know I eat healthy every chance I get."

"Except when you're in the mood for pie."

Edward swallowed a grin. "Yeah. Except then."

The waitress came and took their order, along with their menus, leaving them free to concentrate on one another.

"So," Tracy said, sipping from her glass of ice water, "what's this really about?"

Edward raised his eyebrows. "What do you mean? I just wanted some dessert, and I wanted someone to share it with."

"Uh-huh. Right. Tell that to someone who believes you."

He felt his cheeks warm as he searched for a quick comeback. He couldn't find one.

"All right," he said. "I'll admit it. I just wasn't ready to go home and stare at the ceiling, but I knew Mazie was tired and wanted to get some sleep. She's carrying most of the load as Mimi's caregiver now, you know."

Tracy nodded. "No easy task, is it? How's she holding up?"

"Okay, I guess. They're very close—Mazie and Mimi."

"I noticed. Sometimes I think Mazie's closer to her great-grandmother than to you."

The words hung in the air between them, and Edward wished he could shoot down her premise with conviction. But there were times he thought the same thing.

Before he could decide how to respond, the waitress was back with their pie, and Edward used it as an excuse to let the conversation drop. They could pick it up later, but not along the same lines.

"Is she getting any closer?" Tracy asked between bites.

Edward looked up and frowned.

"Closer to making a commitment," Tracy added.

Edward clenched his teeth. Maybe inviting his sister out for pie hadn't been such a good idea after all. She had such a determined way of poking her nose into his business.

"We're doing just fine," he said, wishing his defensive tone wasn't so obvious.

"That's not what I asked you."

"I know it's not," he said at last, "but it's all I'm going to say about it for now."

Their eyes locked for a moment, until Tracy finally dropped her gaze and returned to eating her pie. Edward did the same, but somehow it just didn't taste as good as he'd expected.

Mazie had flipped over in bed so many times she was tangled in her sheets and despairing of ever falling asleep. No matter how many times she punched her pillow, she just couldn't get comfortable. She'd been yawning by the time Edward left after their second cup of tea, and she thought surely she'd be asleep within moments of climbing into bed. Now, two hours later, she decided to give up and go to the kitchen once again.

Stopping to check on Mimi along the way, she was pleased to see the old woman was sleeping peacefully, even though her TV played softly in the background. *At least one of us is getting some rest.*

As she approached the kitchen, she was surprised to see the light on. Had she forgotten to flip it off before she went to bed?

Stepping inside she found her mother sitting at the table, a mug in front of her.

"What are you doing up?" Mazie asked.

Lilly smiled. "I was just about to ask you the same thing."

Mazie shrugged. "I don't know. Just can't sleep, I guess."

"Me neither." She lifted her cup and started to stand. "I'm having some warm milk. Why don't you try a little? There's still some in the pot, and I don't think it's had time to cool off yet. Here, let me get it for you."

Mazie held up her hand. "Stay put, Mom. I'll get it."

In moments, she had joined her mother at the table, her hands wrapped around her own warm mug. She'd never cared much for warm milk, so she'd stirred a little chocolate syrup into it.

"The caffeine in the chocolate will probably defeat the purpose," her mother warned.

Mazie smiled but ignored the comment. "So how was work today?"

"Ridiculously busy. But that's a good thing, right? I've missed several days of work lately, so I need to make up for the lost cash flow."

Mazie nodded. She knew her mother didn't realize how her comment heaped guilt on Mazie for not being able to contribute to the family budget right now. Her teaching job would start soon, and then she could at least throw a little into the pot, though most would go to help pay off her college loans.

"How was Mimi tonight?" Lilly asked, changing the subject.

Mazie smiled, glad to move the conversation away from finances. "She did really well. She told us about how Harriet found out she and her brothers were going to be sold, and how if that happened she'd probably never see her husband or parents or siblings again. That's what convinced her she had to make her escape to the North. Mimi drifted off before she could tell us if Harriet was able to convince her husband to join her."

Lilly raised her eyebrows. "I can't imagine him staying behind, can you? Or expecting Harriet not to escape, knowing what would happen if she stayed." She shook her head. "We think we have problems sometimes, don't we? But we don't even begin to know what a hard life is until we hear about someone like Harriet Tubman and all she went through. What an amazing woman."

Mazie nodded, finding herself wishing she had just a pinch of Harriet's courage. Here was a woman who knew she could lose everything—her husband, her family, her very life—if she didn't successfully follow her dream for freedom. Even if she did, there was a chance she could lose them all anyway. Mazie, on the other hand, seemed unable even to make a commitment to spend her life with a man who loved and respected her, and whom she was at least relatively certain she loved in return. Oh, if only she could find some answers by the time Mimi's story about the Moses quilt was done!

The alarm pulled Mazie from a deep sleep, wiping out the memory of a vivid dream and forcing her back into the reality of a new day.

Thursday. She squinted into the gray light of her room. *Mom's going into work early, so I'd better get up and get breakfast going for Mimi. If she isn't already awake, she will be soon.*

Reluctant to leave the comfortable warmth of her bed, she nearly dragged herself to the door and out into the hallway, headed for the bathroom. The light was once again on in the kitchen, so she knew her mother was already up and would listen for Mimi while Mazie showered. Then she'd be ready to take over for the day.

By the time she stood under the hot water, letting it stream over her head and rinse out the shampoo, she was awake, planning her day. She'd heard the weatherman say it would be warm and sunny, so if Mimi was up to it, Mazie decided she'd bundle her up and take her out for a walk in her wheelchair. She knew her great-grandmother would complain, as she always did, about being cold, claiming she hadn't been warm since leaving Prattville. But Mazie also knew there was nothing Mimi liked more than getting outside where she could smell the flowers and breathe the clean, fresh air.

Mazie was dressed, with her hair done, in under thirty minutes. Making a beeline for Mimi's room, she peeked inside and found the old woman sleeping. Part of her was relieved, but another part knew her beloved great-grandmother was sleeping far too much these days, spending much more time asleep than awake. Would she simply fall asleep one day soon and not wake up?

The thought sent spikes of fear racing up her spine, prickling her skin as she turned away and closed Mimi's door behind her before heading down the hallway to retrieve some of the delicious-smelling coffee that beckoned her. Knowing her mother would be sitting at the table, praying and reading her Bible before heading off to work, Mazie determined to keep the conversation upbeat. Her mother had enough to deal with. She didn't need a moody, insecure daughter on top of everything else.

Smile in place, she stepped into the kitchen to greet her mother.

CHAPTER TWENTY

Edward stopped to pick up Chinese food on the way to Mazie's that evening. She'd told him it was Mimi's special request, and he'd been happy to oblige. Though she was still on a bit of a restricted diet, it seemed she could have the egg drop soup and possibly a little rice and veggies besides. Mazie had also told him she didn't have much of an appetite anymore, but when she was able to eat, she insisted it be something "with taste." He smiled at the thought, having no problem picturing Mimi saying such a thing.

The sun was just beginning to set when he parked in the driveway and gathered up the bag full of steaming offerings to take inside. It had been exceptionally warm that day, at least for their usually cool corner of the world, and he was glad Mazie and Lilly wouldn't have to heat up the house unnecessarily by cooking. He wondered if Mimi would be up to sitting in her wheelchair and joining them at the kitchen table. He hoped so. It was hard to imagine having to spend nearly all day and night in bed, regardless of how old or weak you might be.

Edward climbed the porch and lifted his hand to ring the bell, but the door opened before he could press the buzzer.

His raised his eyebrows, and he let out a low whistle at the sight of Mazie standing there in a breezy pink sundress, her curly dark hair pulled on top of her head and her cheeks flushed. "Just when I think you can't possibly get any more beautiful than you already are, you show up looking like that."

Mazie's face flushed, and she chuckled—then immediately changed the subject. "Right on time," she said, pushing the screen door open and stepping back to let him come inside.

He leaned down to kiss her. "You know I'd never be late when I have a chance to spend time with you."

Her cheeks flushed a shade darker, and she smiled. "You always know exactly what to say, don't you?"

Edward laughed. "Hardly. But every now and then I do okay." He walked past her into the kitchen and set the bulging bag on the table. "Where's your mom?" he asked, turning back toward Mazie.

"Not home yet. She's still putting in as many hours as possible to make up for the time she missed when Mimi was in the hospital. I called and told her you were bringing dinner, though, so she's already looking forward to it. I imagine she'll be home in a couple of hours."

"So how's Mimi doing today? Is she going to be able to come out here and join us for dinner?"

Mazie nodded. "I think so. For a little while, at least. I don't know how much she'll eat, but she's excited about having Chinese food again and already looking forward to telling us more of her story."

"Good. I'm looking forward to it too. So do you want me to set the table while you get her, or should I be her escort?"

"You know you're her favorite." Mazie grinned. "She adores you. Go ahead and bring her in. I've already got her sitting up in bed with her robe on, so all you have to do is get her into the wheelchair."

"I'm on it." He paused and kissed her again. "You are absolutely gorgeous, you know that?"

Mazie's giggle sounded nervous. "I'm glad you think so. But gorgeous? That's a powerful adjective."

"It fits you." He pushed a loose curl back from her forehead. "I just wish there were a stronger one because gorgeous doesn't do you justice."

For just a moment, she seemed to be at a loss for words. Then she reached up and laid her hand against his cheek. "You are something else, Edward Clayton. I just wonder what I ever did to deserve you." She smiled. "Now go get Mimi before the soup gets cold, will you? We can pick up with the mushy stuff again later."

He returned her smile, wanting to say so much more but knowing he dared not push her. Putting his feelings on hold, he turned away and walked down the hall toward Mimi's room.

Lilly still hadn't made it home by the time they finished eating and got Mimi back into bed. Mazie worried that her great-grandmother might be too tired to give them another installment of her story that night, but the feisty lady insisted otherwise.

"I'm just fine," she said, propped up once again on her pillows, the light from her bed stand illuminating her pale skin. From where Mazie stood, she could count the blue veins standing out on Mimi's trembling hands. She grew weaker by the day—the hour—and Mazie didn't want to push if Mimi was too tired to tell the story. Yet, she also felt an urgency to find out as much about Harriet Tubman as possible—while there was still time.

"Just get me my quilt," Mimi said. "We'll continue where we left off last night, with Harriet knowing her time had come to make her escape—with or without her husband or family."

Mazie brought the Moses quilt and held it up. "Same patch for tonight's story?" she asked.

Mimi nodded. "Yes. The bird flying free of its cage at last." She smiled. "Sit down, you two. You're going to love this part of the story."

Situated in their chairs, Mazie and Edward turned their attention to the frail old woman and waited.

Harriet was heartbroken. Though as determined as ever to escape slavery and knowing with certainty now was the time she had to make her move, she could hardly believe her beloved husband still refused to go with her. If anything, when she told him she had to go so she wouldn't be sold on the auction block, meaning an end to their life together, he became more obstinate in his refusal to join her. He told her it was too dangerous and there simply wasn't anything they could do to change the system of slavery so entrenched in the South.

That answer wasn't good enough for Harriet. Even his threats to expose her if she tried to run weren't enough to stop her from moving ahead with her plan. Her spirit had been set free when she began a deep and personal relationship with God when she was a young girl. Now she was determined to see her physical self set free as well— or die trying. She also believed with all her heart that God had called her to lead as many of her people as possible to freedom. If John Tubman wasn't willing to be one of them, then so be it.

"There's two things I got a right to," Harriet told herself, "and these are death and liberty. One or the other I mean to have ... No one will take me back alive; I shall fight for my liberty, and when the time has come for me to go, the Lord will let them kill me."

She'd known all along she had to be stealthy in making and carrying out her plan, but it was even more dangerous now her own husband was threatening to expose her. Harriet met secretly with her two brothers who were also to be sold and made sure they understood they were to say nothing to John Tubman. They agreed, and the three of them finalized their plans to head north.

Finally, one warm summer evening in the summer of 1849, Harriet wrapped a tiny bit of food in a bandanna, knowing it might be all she'd have for some time. Excitement swirled with sadness inside her, as she wrestled with the need to run and the tragedy of leaving loved ones behind. But she knew the time had come—her escape could not be delayed any longer. Sadly, she couldn't even risk telling her parents or other siblings what was about to happen the next morning. She and her two brothers would simply have to slip off unnoticed without bidding farewell to anyone.

Harriet did, however, find a way to leave a message behind, one that her family and friends would understand once they realized Harriet and her brothers were gone. As her final day on the plantation ended, Harriet walked through the slave quarters, singing as she so often did. But the words to the Negro spiritual she had chosen were not without deep meaning.

I'm sorry, friends, to leave you,
Farewell! oh, farewell!
But I'll meet you in the morning,
Farewell! oh, farewell!
I'll meet you in the morning,
When you reach the Promised Land;
On the other side of Jordan,
For I'm bound for the Promised Land.

Before morning dawned over the plantation or anyone in the slave quarters was stirring, Harriet and her brothers had stolen into the darkness, taking their first steps on a long and perilous journey. It was, in fact, so perilous that Harriet's brothers soon turned back, leaving her to complete her flight to freedom alone.

And yet Harriet knew she was not alone. "Oh, dear Lord," she prayed, "I ain't got no friend but you. Come to my help, Lord, for I'm in trouble."

And so Harriet Tubman, bereft of family, friends, and finances, pressed on—accompanied only by her God and destined to become the Moses of her people.

CHAPTER TWENTY-ONE

"Mimi?"

Mazie waited, hoping her great-grandmother's eyes would flutter open and she would continue with her story. After a moment or two, she realized that was not going to happen.

"I think she's done for the night," Edward whispered.

Mazie nodded, glad for the warmth of his hand as he wrapped it around hers. "You're right. We'll just have to wait to find out what happens next."

They were out in the hallway before Edward responded. "I should already know," he said. "What happened next, I mean. We studied Harriet Tubman in school, and you'd think I'd have realized how important her life was and tried a little harder to retain more of the facts."

"We studied it too," Mazie said as they turned their steps toward the family room where a dim antique lamp greeted them. They settled next to one another on the plush couch, Edward sitting on one end and Mazie beside him. "But I have to admit I really don't remember much about her at all. I knew she was known as the Moses of her people and she was involved with the Underground Railroad, leading slaves to freedom, but that's about it. Somehow, listening to Mimi's story and following it on her quilt makes it more ... personal, I suppose. Don't you think?"

Edward wrapped his arms around her and pulled her back against his chest. "Absolutely," he agreed. "And I have to admit I'm really kind of anxious to hear the rest of the story. Do you think she's strong enough to finish telling it?"

Mazie drew her eyebrows together. She certainly wanted to believe it, but she had her doubts. "I hope so," she whispered, hating the hot sting of tears that pricked her eyes. "I really do hope so. I know one thing for sure, though. She'll give it her best try."

Though she couldn't see Edward's face, she could hear the smile in his voice. "That's for sure. Your Mimi is one strong, feisty lady. Reminds me of Harriet Tubman in some ways." He chuckled. "I wouldn't be surprised to find out she was descended from her."

Mazie's laugh escaped from a nervous stomach, the possibilities of Edward's words poking holes in an invisible wall she hadn't even realized she'd erected around her heart. It was impossible, of course. Mimi couldn't possibly be descended from Harriet Tubman. And yet, there was something, some nugget of truth in Edward's statement that niggled at questions Mazie had long suppressed, questions about her family that had never been really answered or addressed. Was it possible Mimi was telling them this story about the Moses quilt so their family could finally unwrap a story of their own?

It seemed too far-fetched to be true, but Mazie tucked the thought away in a corner of her heart, waiting to see if her great-grandmother might find a way to dig it back out and force her to deal with it at last. Perhaps then she might be able to move on and grapple with the issues that held her back from giving Edward the answer she knew he longed to hear.

Friday evening once again found Mazie and Edward at Mimi's bedside, anxiously awaiting the next portion of her story. Lilly had come home early and joined them all for dinner—beef stew that Mazie had simmered in a crock pot throughout the day—and had now retired to her room to watch some TV and unwind before heading into work early the next morning. Weekends were always her busiest time.

Still focusing on the bird-flying-free-from-its-cage patch, Mimi offered a wan smile before taking them back to Harriet's dangerous journey away from those she loved and into the unknown.

Harriet, it seems, had first heard of the Underground Railroad when she was still a child. Tales of those who helped runaway slaves along the way had fueled her passion for freedom. Many evenings, after the slaves had finished their work for the day, they huddled together and shared their stories in whispers, knowing they could get in trouble just talking about escape. But Harriet had listened intently, learning about the variety of routes the slaves used and how they contacted those who would help them in their efforts. Harriet heard how difficult and arduous the journey was and how many failed to complete it. But that didn't dissuade her. She concentrated instead on those who made it to the North, where it was said they were free to live as they wished, serving no master but the Lord God himself. She'd long believed it was a goal worth striving for, even if she lost her life in the process. She had even had dreams throughout the years of a line drawn across the country that separated free people from slaves. In her dreams, she also saw white women, beckoning her with smiles to come and join them. Harriet firmly believed those dreams were from God.

Harriet, of course, had no idea she would be one of an estimated hundred thousand slaves who successfully made that journey on the Underground Railroad, escaping to the North and establishing a life for themselves, free from slavery. This was no easy feat. In addition to walking countless miles on foot, through treacherous terrain and terrible weather, the fugitive slave statute, passed by Congress in 1793, allowed owners to recapture their slaves and bring them back to their plantations, punishing them in any way they saw fit. That any made it through at all speaks highly of the slaves' courage and determination, as well as God's sovereign intervention on their behalf.

And that was the key for Harriet. If she hadn't firmly believed God had called her to escape for the purpose of later helping others do the same, and the Lord Himself would protect and guide her in the process, she would have been foolish at best to move ahead with her plans.

For years, Harriet had heard slaves could live free in Philadelphia or New York. With her faith fixed firmly on God, she set her mind to reach one of the two cities, although she had no compass or map, no money and almost no food, and worst of all, knowing her own husband had no doubt sounded the alarm when he awoke that morning and realized she had fled.

Harriet set out with one immediate destination, a flimsy hope but the only earthly one she had. She had once met a White woman, a Quaker named Miss Parsons, while working in the fields. When the woman noticed the strange scar on Harriet's forehead, she had stopped to ask about it.

Harriet told the story of helping the slave escape and being hit in the head when her master tossed the lead weight to try to stop him. She also revealed the health issues she'd had as a result. Apparently, Miss Parsons was touched by her story and told Harriet if there was ever anything she could do to help her she should not hesitate to ask.

That fragile promise now echoed in Harriet's memory as she started off on her journey, praying she correctly remembered the woman's directions to her farm. Thankfully, she did. Thankfully too, Miss Parsons also remembered Harriet and was a woman of her word. It was Harriet's first experience with the Underground Railroad.

Miss Parsons fed Harriet and told her of two stops to make on her way north, assuring her she would find people in both places who would help her. Harriet waited until dark to strike out again, following the North Star as she trudged along the bank of the Choptank River. When clouds covered the stars, she rubbed her hands on trees until she found the moss that grew on the north side of their trunks.

She arrived at the first stop at daybreak. By afternoon, she was bumping along in a wagon, hidden under blankets. Despite the rough ride and continued danger, she quickly gave in to exhaustion and fell asleep.

At the next stop, she received more food and more instructions and soon continued on her way, progressing ever northward, traveling only at night and always staying off the main roads. From one stop to another, she made it all the way to Wilmington, Delaware, where she met a man who would soon become a close friend and partner in rescuing other slaves.

The man's name was Thomas Garrett, and he was already deeply involved in the Underground Railroad when Harriet appeared in his life. A devout Quaker, he had dedicated his life to rescuing slaves and seeing slavery abolished. That Thomas and Harriet connected at this point was, in Harriet's mind, one more sign God had indeed called her to escape and to become involved in helping others do the same.

With the help and direction of Thomas Garrett and others, Harriet spent several days hidden in the attic of a Quaker home, as well as in the haystack of a German immigrant and a dark hole that a free Black family used to store their potatoes. From there, she took one last wagon ride north before stepping over the Pennsylvania line into freedom.

Freedom. The word nearly took Harriet's breath away. Could it be true? Had she really made it?

"I looked at my hands to see if I was the same person, now that I was free," Harriet recalled later. "There was such a glory over everything. The sun came up like gold through the trees and over the fields, and I felt like I was in Heaven."

Harriet had successfully escaped from slavery. Technically, she was free. But a myriad of questions remained to be answered. With no money, no education, and no friends or family to turn to, how and where would she live? That seemed the biggest challenge, the greatest question at that point, and so she resolved to seek God for the answer.

With Mimi once again drifting off to sleep and Lilly assuring them she could handle things without them, Edward and Mazie slipped out the front door and climbed into Edward's convertible. Though the day had been exceptionally warm, the sun had long since set and darkness brought cooler temperatures their way. Mazie was glad she'd grabbed a sweater on the way out—gladder still when Edward volunteered to raise the top on his car.

"Where to?" he asked, placing his key in the ignition.

She shrugged. "I have no idea. I was hoping you might."

He glanced down at her. "There are a million places I'd like to take you—someday." He smiled. "For now, how about a walk on the beach?"

She raised her eyebrows. "You really feel like driving that far?"

"Why not? Tomorrow's Saturday, and I don't have to get up early." He braked before backing into the street. "Oh, wait. Your mom's going in to work early tomorrow, isn't she? That means you'll be on Mimi-duty at sunrise."

"I'm afraid so. Still, that walk on the beach sounds awfully tempting."

"Next time. And we'll plan it better, I promise. For now, how about our favorite ice cream spot? I could go for sharing a sundae."

"Hot fudge? With everything?"

He grinned. "Is there any other kind?"

In less than fifteen minutes, they were sitting across from one another at a jam-packed ice cream parlor. It seemed an event at the high school must have just ended, and the entire student body yearned for ice cream. Mazie knew the only reason they'd gotten a table so quickly was because the owners were Edward's friends.

Seems like everyone is Edward's friend. She gazed across the table at him as the two of them scooped the fudgy dessert from the overflowing bowl. *And why not? What's not to like about him, or love, for that matter? He's good and kind, intelligent and successful—not to mention, extremely handsome. I can only imagine how many women would trade places with me in a heartbeat.*

Edward paused in the middle of their ice cream marathon and said, "So, were you as blown away as I was by tonight's story about Harriet's escape?"

Mazie let the creamy delight slide down her throat before answering. "Absolutely. Mimi really has a way of bringing the story to life, doesn't she? I know I sure wasn't as impressed when I read about it in the history books at school."

"Neither was I. Barely noticed it, to be honest." A flash of regret danced through his dark eyes. "And shame on me for it. Seriously, some of those slaves could have been my ancestors for all I know, and I barely paid attention to what they went through to be free."

Mazie hated the flush she knew had risen from her neck to her cheeks, but she couldn't stop it. Edward was right, of course, and he wasn't saying anything she hadn't known all along. And yet, for some reason, she felt as if he'd drawn a line of division between them by saying it.

Or was it just her imagination, playing havoc with her thoughts as it so often did? That, added to her insecurities and other idiosyncrasies, could easily account for what she was feeling now.

Shoving the unnamed feelings down where so many others had accumulated over the years, she forced a smile and shoveled another spoonful of vanilla ice cream and fudge into her mouth. She was glad for the shared dessert that gave her an excuse for not responding directly to Edward's comment, but she didn't kid herself he hadn't noticed her omission. His dark eyes were far too easy to read. He wanted so much more from her than she was able to give. Would it always be that way? She prayed not, but the answers she believed could one day set her free continued to elude her.

CHAPTER TWENTY-TWO

By late Saturday morning, Mimi announced she was again up to sharing another part of Harriet's story if anyone was interested in hearing it. Mazie called Edward, who came right over, deli sandwiches in hand. After a quick lunch, they settled in to hear what Mimi had to say.

One of the first people Harriet met after arriving in Philadelphia was a man named William Still. Harriet believed that once again God had intervened to connect the two of them, for she had prayed, "Oh, dear Lord, I ain't got no friend but you. Come to my help, Lord, for I'm in trouble?"

William Still was deeply involved with the rescue of slaves and even headed the Philadelphia Vigilance Committee, a group that helped Harriet find a place to live as well as a job. Harriet too became active in the committee, spending many evenings in their offices, listening and learning more about the activities of the Underground Railroad, fueling her passion to go back to the South and begin rescuing other slaves.

As Harriet settled into her new life, she spent the first year working as a cleaning woman, a cook, a laundress, and a seamstress. She didn't have much personal time, but she was so thrilled to be free she didn't mind long hours of work one bit. She did, however, save every penny she could, as she planned to use it to finance her trips to the South. Though she knew what it could mean if she were caught, she didn't let fear of repercussions dissuade her. God had freed her for a purpose, and she trusted Him to guide her into the fulfillment of that purpose—at any cost. Harriet was fearless when she believed she was acting in God's will and, therefore, under His protection.

"In point of courage, shrewdness, and disinterested exertion to rescue her fellowmen," William Still said of Harriet, "by making personal visits into Maryland among the slaves, she was without equal. And it is probable, was never known before or since."

In December of 1850, just over one year after making her own escape, Harriet got word that some of her family members had escaped to Baltimore. One of her sisters, along with her sister's husband and two children were tantalizingly close. Now they needed help to make it the rest of the way.

Praying and believing God would lead and protect her, Harriet struck out on her first rescue mission. She was successful, connecting with them and bringing them back to the safety of Philadelphia. Not long after that, she snuck back into enemy territory and brought back one of her brothers and two other men.

Harriet Tubman's line of the Underground Railroad was officially open for business. She made trips as often as circumstances allowed, leading slaves to safety in either Philadelphia or New York. And yet, though this woman who was quickly becoming known as "Moses" was heroic, she did not take foolish chances. She went when and where she believed God directed her, trusting Him to keep her safe until her work for Him was done.

Harriet had great success in bringing slaves to freedom, despite seemingly insurmountable odds. Included in those she helped escape were her aging parents and some of her siblings. But the one person she was unable to bring with her was the one she wanted so desperately to join her: John Tubman, her husband.

From the time of her escape in 1849, she had dreamed of going back for John so they could resume their life together up north. Finally, in the fall of 1851, she dressed as a man and made her way back to the old slave quarters where she had lived with her beloved before her escape. It was her third trip back to Maryland, and she was determined not to leave without seeing John and trying to convince him to come with her.

Sadly, when she sent a messenger to tell him she had returned, John refused to see her. Some accounts say John had remarried and started a new life with someone else. Whether or not that was true, Harriet was forced once more to leave the man she loved behind. She finally let him go in her heart, knowing she had to continue without him.

The trip wasn't a failure, however. Harriet managed to gather eleven willing slaves, including one of her brothers and his family, and she escorted them on a fifteen-hundred-mile trip north, all the way to the safety of Canada, where slavery had already been abolished.

Harriet "Moses" Tubman was now wanted, dead or alive, and stories vary as to how much of a bounty was placed on her head. And yet she continued to successfully bring slaves to freedom, depending on her shrewdness and courage, assistance from other abolitionists—and most of all, her unswerving faith in God.

"Oh, Mimi, what a beautiful story," Mazie breathed as Mimi finished the last of her tale. "I'm so glad you told us about Harriet Tubman." She frowned then and glanced at the quilt, lying open on her great-grandmother's bed. "But ... there are so many patches left. Is there more about her life that we don't know yet?"

Mimi chuckled, coughing a bit before she was done and then pausing to catch her breath. At last she said, "Child, you haven't even begun to hear all that Harriet Tubman did in her lifetime. All I've told you so far is the part about her life as a slave and then her work to help lead others to freedom. There is so much more to this amazing woman, and I can't wait to tell you about it." She paused again, breathing as deeply as she was able. "But for now I must rest. I'll tell you more tonight—after dinner." She smiled and darted her eyes from Mazie to Edward and back again. "So stick around, will you?"

Mazie and Edward agreed and quietly let themselves out of the room so Mimi could get some rest.

Edward and Mazie sat on the front porch, watching the afternoon fog creep across the valley below, even as warm sunshine continued to blanket the two of them.

"Are you sure you're up for another chapter of Mimi's story this evening?" Mazie asked, sipping her unsweetened iced tea.

"Absolutely." Edward downed the contents of his own glass and set it on the small redwood table between them.

"I wouldn't miss it." He turned toward her. "I do have a special request for tomorrow, though."

Mazie raised her eyebrows. "Sure. What is it?"

"Mom and Dad asked if I'd like to bring you over for Sunday dinner after church. Their service lets out about an hour after yours, so we can go to either one and then head on over there. What do you think? Would your mom be up to staying with Mimi in the afternoon?"

"That won't be a problem." Mazie sighed. "Mom just told me this morning she's arranged for a caregiver to come tomorrow, so she and I will both be free to go to church. Mimi's just getting too weak to go. Last week nearly did her in, I'm afraid."

Edward's dark eyes misted over, wrenching Mazie's heart at the reminder he loved not only her but her entire family. He took her hand and caressed it with his thumb. "I'm so sorry, baby. I know how hard this is on you."

Mazie nodded, forcing down the lump in her throat until she trusted herself to speak. "Mom already mentioned the caregiver can stay as long as necessary, though I don't think Mom has any special plans and will probably just come home and take over after church."

"Mimi's not going to like missing church."

A smile touched Mazie's lips. "You're right about that. But even she admitted that last week was too much for her. I keep hoping she'll regain her strength, but Mom says that's not likely."

They sat in silence for a moment, as Edward continued to rub the back of Mazie's hand. A waft of breeze teased her nostrils with the sweet fragrance of roses, now in full bloom in the front yard. Somehow, it seemed odd to her that life should go on around her even as her great-grandmother's time on earth was coming to an end. She knew Mimi would breathe her last and go straight into the presence of the Lord she had loved and served for so many years, but that didn't ease the ache that had been growing in Mazie's heart.

"Is there anything I can bring tomorrow? Your mom and Tracy are such good cooks that I can't begin to compete, but I could contribute a salad or something."

"It's not necessary. But if you want to, sure. A salad is always good."

Mazie nodded, leaned her head back, and closed her eyes. She needed these peaceful moments with Edward, and she truly was looking forward to spending some time with his family again. They'd become part of the many people and things she'd neglected lately, as Mimi's health failed. She was grateful Edward was so understanding about her priorities right now, though she knew when Mimi was gone she would have to reexamine them once and for all.

CHAPTER TWENTY-THREE

Mazie was haunted by the idea Harriet Tubman was so driven to find freedom she left her husband behind. She wondered if she would ever experience a passion or longing so deep she would be willing to risk absolutely everything else to achieve it. She also wondered how much deeper Harriet's feelings for John Tubman had run than her feelings for Edward.

She and Edward, along with Lilly and Mimi, who had joined them briefly in her wheelchair, had shared a light supper of soup and sandwiches, and now they were all gathered around Mimi's bed, ready to continue the saga of this courageous woman. Mazie had been surprised when even Lilly had decided to join them, but when she heard Mimi was going to tell them about Harriet's life beyond rescuing slaves on the Underground Railroad, she'd quickly voiced her interest.

"I had no idea there was more to Harriet's story than slave rescues," she'd said. "After all, that's enough to make her a legend, and as far as I can remember, that's all I learned about her in school. I'd really like to know more."

And so the three of them sat at Mimi's bedside, the quilt open beside the old woman as the dying rays of sun peeked through the large window and kept the room comfortably warm.

Mimi smiled at them. "How lovely to have all three of you here with me," she said, her voice trembling a bit. "I'm glad you're all here to learn about this great woman and the many things she did in her long and busy life." She smiled. "Mazie, hold up the Moses quilt, will you?"

Mazie did, waiting for her great-grandmother's next instruction.

"You see that gold coin there, off to the right?"

Mazie looked and pointed when she'd found it.

"Yes, child, that's it. That coin represents the many expenses involved in supporting Harriet's treks back and forth to the South, not to mention her own living expenses and caring for her aging parents and others once she'd brought them north. This uneducated woman, who remained nearly penniless her entire life, carried a lot of responsibility on her shoulders, but between her willingness to work hard at any task put before her and her complete reliance on a faithful God, her needs were always met, one way or another. Why, in 1857, she was even able to purchase a home from her close friend and ardent abolitionist, William Seward—who, as you know, also went on to become Abraham Lincoln's secretary of state. She turned that house into a refuge for herself and her aging parents, as well as others from time to time, who just needed a roof over their heads. And somehow, some way, she also managed to keep food on the table."

Mimi shook her head and let her gaze pass from one to the other of her listeners. "Besides receiving donations from other abolitionists and supporters of her work—sometimes miraculously—Harriet supplemented her cleaning and washerwoman income in some surprising ways."

Harriet had been attending antislavery events for years, but when approached in 1858 to become a speaker, she was stunned. Who would want to listen to an uneducated former slave, she wondered. Her presence, however, was already well established in such circles. Historian William Wells said this about her:

> For eight or ten years previous to the breaking out of the Rebellion, all who frequented anti-slavery conventions, lectures, picnics, and fairs, could not fail to have seen a black woman of medium size, upper front teeth gone, smiling countenance, attired in coarse, but neat apparel, with an old-fashioned reticule or bag suspended by her side, and who, on taking her seat, would at once drop off into a sound sleep.

Harriet continued to suffer the effects of the injury she'd sustained at the hands of her former master when she was young, yet it didn't deter her efforts to rescue slaves or to provide support for those who depended on her. As a result, when urged to join the speaking circuit, she sought God's guidance and decided it was indeed what He wanted her to do.

As it turned out, Harriet proved to be an eloquent speaker, moving her listeners with her emotion-filled, firsthand accounts of the brutality and evil of slavery. However, because there was such a high price on her head, she had to conceal her identity. A minister friend of hers named Thomas Wentworth Higginson first introduced her to the audience as "Moses," alluding to her work of leading the slaves to freedom, much as the biblical Moses led the Israelites out of Egypt. Though she occasionally used other names to protect her identity, the name Moses seemed to fit her and stayed with her even after her death.

Harriet's appearances on the speaking circuit, even under cover of an alias, catapulted her even farther into New England's elite society. Amazed, Harriet soon found herself invited into the homes of such prominent White people as Amos Bronson Alcott, father of Louisa May Alcott, Mrs. Horace Mann, and Ralph Waldo Emerson, all of whom quickly developed a deep and abiding respect for the former slave woman. Her friend Reverend Higginson referred to Harriet as "the greatest heroine of the age"

Harriet was unchanged by such praise and admiration. The humble woman with the heart of a lion still went home, bone weary at the end of the day, and thanked God for getting her through once again. When she awoke in the morning, she offered Him praise and presented her petitions to Him, fully expecting Him to answer in the way He knew best. Because of her complete dependence on God, she didn't hesitate when asked to expand her public speaking to include the cause of women's suffrage. As a result, Harriet quickly became acquainted with such prominent women as Elizabeth Cady Stanton, Lucretia Mott, and Susan B. Anthony. Though Harriet didn't seek to cultivate these relationships, nor did she expect to benefit from them, she was pleased when God used these women to help fund Harriet's work as well as the home she maintained for her parents and others.

Finally, toward the end of 1860, Harriet made her last trip back to Maryland, where she rescued a family of five. It wasn't until February of 1861 that she finally delivered that small group of slaves, safe and sound, to their destination in New York City. That spring, the Civil War erupted, and Harriet's life changed once again.

The next morning Edward and Mazie opted to attend church with Lilly, not wanting her to have to go alone. Edward drove, bringing Lilly home immediately following the service. After checking in on Mimi, whose caregiver was about to turn the still sleeping elderly woman over to Lilly's care, Mazie grabbed her pineapple and cabbage salad from the refrigerator and followed Edward out to his car.

"Mom and Dad will be so glad to see you," he said, as he opened the door for her.

"I'll be glad to see them too," Mazie said. "It's been way too long since I've spent any time with them."

"That's what Mom was saying the other day." Edward started the car and looked over his shoulder as he backed up. "They're crazy about you, you know."

Mazie felt her cheeks warm. "I know," she said, wishing she could say more. She enjoyed being around Edward's family, Tracy included, but she just couldn't seem to let her shield down and enjoy them thoroughly.

She peeked at Edward, who was now straightening out the car and heading down the street toward his parents' place. His eyes were straight ahead, but she knew from the flicker of movement in his jaw he was holding back words he wanted to say.

"So ... how have your parents been anyway? Busy as ever?"

Edward laughed. "Are you kidding? Dad is always working, and Mom is totally involved at church—except when she's busy looking for a potential husband for Tracy." He glanced at her and winked before turning back to the road. "Tracy does her best to ignore her, but she knows only too well how happy Mom would be if she'd get married and have kids. Seems Mom has dreamed of being a grandmother since Tracy and I were little."

Mazie forced a smile. No doubt his mother's dream included Edward's future as a husband and father as well, and Mazie wasn't being very cooperative in making that dream come true. She stifled a sigh, hoping she hadn't made a mistake by agreeing to spend the afternoon with Edward's family.

Tracy met them at the door as they climbed the porch steps. "There they are," she announced, loudly enough so her parents could hear.

Mazie smiled and stepped into Tracy's outstretched arms, returning the embrace. She truly did like Edward's sister and wanted to be close to her. If she could only get past her insecurities and make the commitment.

"Mazie!"

Barbara Clayton appeared in the doorway, just behind Tracy. Her creamy brown skin glowed as she stepped forward to transfer Mazie from Tracy's arms into her own. "You're finally here! We have missed you, girl."

"I've missed you too," Mazie said, surprised at the truth of her words. "How are you, Mrs. Clayton?"

Barbara tsk-tsked and pulled back to eye Mazie with raised eyebrows. "Now how many times have I told you not to call me Mrs. Clayton? For heaven's sake, we're practically family now. You can call me Barbara, or Mom if you'd like— which would be just fine with me."

Mazie smiled. "You're right. Mrs. Clayton is a bit formal, isn't it?"

"I should say so," Barbara agreed with a laugh, turning from Mazie to her son and reaching up to give him a hug and kiss. Mazie was relieved at the distraction. At least she hadn't been pinned down to choose between Barbara and Mom.

In moments, they were all inside, inhaling the delicious aroma wafting from the kitchen. Despite herself, Mazie found her mouth watering.

"Oh, Mom—" Edward said, heading straight toward the source of the tantalizing smell, "—did you make what I think you made?"

Barbara laughed, a rich, warm sound that made Mazie feel even more welcome. "I surely did," she said, following her son. "That roast has been in the oven since early this morning, and it's so tender I think we'll have to drink it with a straw."

Mazie's smile widened as she and Tracy joined the others in the kitchen. Barbara opened the oven door so they could enjoy the full impact of the aroma, and in moments, John Clayton came in behind them.

"That's it," he said. "I can't take smelling that any longer without at least getting a taste of it. Cut me off a slice, Barb."

"I will not," she teased. "You can wait like everyone else. It'll all be ready and on the table within the hour."

John groaned, then turned his attention to Mazie and winked. "You see how they treat me around here?" he asked, taking her shoulders and pulling her in for a hug and a kiss on the forehead. "How are you, young lady? It's about time my son brought you over to see me."

Mazie smiled up at the man who was an absolute double of his son—plus a few years and gray hairs. She knew she could look at John Clayton and visualize exactly what Edward would look like in a couple of decades. *Still handsome.* She watched as father and son engaged in a bit of hugging and backslapping before they all adjourned to the family room.

It would be a good visit, she decided, glad after all she'd agreed to come. The next installment of the Moses quilt story could wait until Edward brought her home in the evening. For now, she would relax and enjoy the warmth and love of this very kind family who so completely accepted her just as she was.

CHAPTER TWENTY-FOUR

"I believe I'd like to sit in the kitchen for our storytelling time tonight," Mimi announced, as she sat up in bed, finishing her meager attempt at consuming a small amount of supper. "I'm tired of looking at these four walls. Besides, I'd enjoy a cup of tea around the table while I tell you about some of Harriet's other adventures."

Lilly raised her eyebrows in surprise but smiled and said, "If that's what you want, Mimi, then that's what we shall do. Edward and Mazie should be back any minute, and then we'll all assemble in the kitchen with the teapot in front of us."

Her response seemed to please the elderly woman, who sighed contentedly as she pushed her food tray away. "I'm done," she said. "Just not very hungry these days, I'm afraid."

Lilly bit her lip to keep from saying anything. After all, what was there to say? Her grandmother was most certainly dying, and the fact she had nearly stopped eating entirely only hastened the process.

Lilly picked up the tray and turned to take it to the kitchen. "I'll be right back," she said. "And then I'll help you get comfortable so you can rest a bit before we go out into the kitchen. Will you be all right for a few minutes?"

Mimi's eyes fluttered closed, and her nod was nearly imperceptible.

Lilly carried the tray into the kitchen, blinking back tears as she walked. Accepting the inevitable was indeed a difficult process.

She'd no sooner scraped off the leftovers and rinsed the plate than she heard the front door open.

"We're home," Mazie called.

"In here," Lilly responded.

She shut off the faucet and turned to greet Edward and Mazie. The sight of them together restored her joy, though she breathed a silent prayer, asking God to bring the breakthrough needed for Mazie to resolve the reservations that held her back from committing to what was so obviously a God-ordained relationship.

"How's Mimi?" Mazie asked as Edward helped her out of her lightweight jacket.

"She didn't eat much," Lilly admitted, "but then that's becoming pretty routine with her, I'm afraid."

Mazie's previously joyous expression faded, and she turned toward the hallway. "I'm going to go check on her."

"She's resting," Lilly said. "But she said she wants to come out here and have tea with all of us while she tells her story this evening."

Mazie stopped and looked back at Lilly, as Edward laid a hand on her arm. "Do you think that's a good idea?" she asked.

"I don't know if it is or not," Lilly admitted, "but it's what she wants. And I think we should honor her wishes if possible, don't you?"

She watched the battle of emotions play across her daughter's face. At last, her shoulders relaxed, and she nodded. "I suppose you're right."

Lilly smiled. "All right then. I told her I'd be right back, so why don't you make the tea, and if she still insists on coming to the kitchen, I'll bring her out."

Edward slipped his arm around Mazie's waist and pulled her close. Lilly's heart warmed when she saw Mazie lean against him. She dried her hands on a dishtowel and returned to her grandmother's room. Within moments, they were all gathered around the table, sipping tea, examining the quilt patch that showed a Union flag, and awaiting the next portion of Mimi's story.

With the outbreak of war between the North and South, Harriet certainly didn't find her workload eased. Though she no longer dared to continue her rescue missions in the same way she'd been doing, she quickly found herself enmeshed in other duties, all of which presented new opportunities to pursue her passions for freedom and justice.

The war was only a few months old when Harriet received a letter from John Andrew, the governor of Massachusetts, requesting her service in the Union Army. Harriet, unable to read the letter herself, listened as the words were read to her, requesting her assistance as nurse, spy, and scout. She would be stationed on the South Carolina coast, in the capacity of emissary between newly freed slaves and their Union liberators.

Harriet was stunned. She was also torn. Her aging parents required her care, including provision for food and shelter. And they weren't the only ones living in her Auburn home. Destitute slaves arrived on her doorstep almost daily, looking for any help she could give them. The weight on her shoulders was already more than most people would even attempt to bear.

After a brief time of prayer, however, she realized there were others who could step in and tend the home fires—including her parents—while she was away. She agreed to the governor's request, though it was May of 1862 before the doors opened for her to become actively involved in the service of the Union Army.

Sailing to the South Carolina Sea Islands on a government transport, Harriet reported directly to Brigadier General David Hunter. Though personally disappointed with President Abraham Lincoln, in that she felt his top priority should be freeing the slaves rather than preventing secession, she committed to doing whatever she could to help the northern cause.

"God won't let Master Lincoln beat the South till he does the right thing," Harriet declared. "Master Lincoln is a great man, and I'm a poor negro, but this negro can tell Master Lincoln how to save money and young men. He can do it by setting the negroes free."

Despite her strong feelings about the president's misplaced priorities, Harriet spent her first months in South Carolina working at the Contraband Hospital in Beaufort under the direction of a surgeon named Henry Durant. The term "contraband" referred to newly freed slaves who worked in a support capacity for the Union Army. The hospital was set up to care for them if they became injured or ill. During this time, some believed Harriet may have received a soldier's pay of fifteen dollars per month, but other stories counter that claim. Some say the Blacks resented the fact Harriet got paid and they didn't, so she gave up her meager salary to help establish a deeper relationship with them. Other stories say she was never paid and had to find a means of supporting herself from the very beginning of her time of service.

Whatever the case, Harriet worked long, hard hours. After exhausting days of ministering to those in the contraband hospital, she labored late into the night as well, baking pies and gingerbread and making root beer, which she then sold to the Union troops. Any money she earned over and above what she needed for her own most basic needs was given over to help Blacks become self-sufficient.

During this time of service, Harriet traveled as far south as Florida, working her way up and down the coast, delivering babies, nursing smallpox victims, tending war wounds, and offering prayer and encouragement everywhere she went. Because she had such complete faith in God and, therefore. no fear of death, she never hesitated to walk into the worst situations imaginable and offer any aid she could.

Nursing wasn't Harriet's only activity. She also served as a spy, employing the knowledge she'd gathered over the years as she slipped back and forth between the North and the South, rescuing slaves from right under their master's nose. The only protection she carried with her was official letters of recommendation, though she did travel with scouts and river pilots, who worked under her direction. Her success as a spy soon came to equal her reputation as a deliverer of slaves. She worked tirelessly for the Union cause for two years, until exhaustion forced her back to her home in Auburn.

After a time of much needed rest, she returned to her service, though this time stationed at Fortress Monroe,

Virginia, where she found the conditions much worse than at her previous post. She was there on April 9, 1865, when the joyous news arrived the war had ended. Sadly, when Harriet boarded a train to head home to New York, the White conductor refused to honor her military pass. The conductor and three other men grabbed Harriet and roughly escorted her to a baggage car where she remained throughout the journey.

The woman who had rescued hundreds of slaves before the war and given three years of her life to serve the Union Army, most likely without any monetary compensation, realized the fight to set her people free was far from over.

"Mimi looked drained when we finally got her into bed," Edward observed, as he and Mazie sat beside one another on the couch in the family room.

"More than usual, I think," Mazie agreed, a sense of growing unease niggling at her heart. Even more than the old woman's obvious physical weakness, Mazie was concerned with the faraway look she'd seen in Mimi's eyes when she tucked her into bed. It was almost as if she were already gone, the remaining flicker of light in her eyes nearly extinguished. But no one else had mentioned it, and she certainly wasn't going to.

"It's funny," Edward said. "I at least remember studying about Harriet Tubman and knowing she was involved with rescuing slaves, but I had no idea she served in the Union Army too."

"Neither did I," Mazie added, snuggling closer against Edward's shoulder. "I can't help but wonder what other causes she was involved in. You heard Mimi say there was still more, right?"

Edward nodded. "I did. And part of me is curious enough that I want to go online and find out everything I can about the woman called Moses." He sighed. "But then I think how much I'd miss by reading it rather than listening to Mimi tell us. Somehow it just seems so much more personal that way."

"Exactly what I was thinking. Maybe after a good night's rest and a quiet day tomorrow, she'll be up to another story." She tilted her head and looked up at him. "How about you? Are you up for another evening over here? Seems we've been monopolizing your time ever since this storytelling started."

Edward grinned down at her. "If it means I get to spend more time with you, I hope the story goes on forever." He kissed the tip of her nose. "Besides, you know I care about Mimi and want to spend as much time with her as I can before—"

Mazie watched the flash of realization cross his face as he caught himself and stopped. She knew what he was about to say, and he was right. But she really didn't want to be reminded of it.

"I'm sorry," he whispered.

She blinked back tears and nodded. "I know. We're running out of time, aren't we?" She closed her eyes and leaned against his chest as he stroked her hair.

CHAPTER TWENTY-FIVE

Mazie awoke with a jerk, her heart thumping hard against her ribcage. What was it? A noise? A feeling? A whisper?

She peeked at the illuminated clock beside her bed. Just a few minutes after four. It wouldn't even start to get light for more than an hour. Mazie had her alarm set for six so she could get up and check on Mimi. Monday was usually Lilly's day off, but Mazie knew her mother had opted to go in to work for the day to help make up for all the time she'd missed. That meant Mazie would be responsible for caring for her great-grandmother all day.

Mimi.

The word echoed as surely as if Mazie had spoken it aloud. She threw back the covers, grabbed her robe from the foot of the bed, and threw it on as she raced from her room to Mimi's.

The house was still and dark, the only sound being the ticking of the mantle clock drifting down the hallway from the family room. Mazie had never realized how loud it was before.

Slowing her pace at Mimi's door, she encircled the knob with her right hand, trying to calm her breathing. At last she turned the knob and pushed the door open, forcing herself to step inside.

Mimi lay as still as ever, her head resting against her favorite pillow. The covers were drawn up to her chin, just as Mazie had left them the night before. Surprisingly the TV wasn't on, and Mazie strained to hear Mimi's breathing as she approached her bed.

Leaning down beside her, she listened, willing herself to feel at least a light puff of air on her cheek. "Mimi?" she whispered at last, turning to gaze into the woman's ashen face.

When Mimi's eyelids fluttered open, Mazie thought her heart would stop. "Mimi," she repeated, louder this time. "Can you hear me? Are you all right?"

Her great-grandmother's eyes appeared glassy, empty—and just as the night before, lifeless and far away. But a smile lifted the edges of her lips as she croaked one word: "Angels."

"Angels?" Mazie frowned. "What about them, Mimi?"

"Singing. Calling my name. Hear them?"

Mazie's heart froze. She didn't like where this was going at all. "I ... don't, Mimi. I'm sorry." She took Mimi's hand in hers and was stunned at how cold it was.

"Going home, child," Mimi rasped, her eyes closing again.

"No, Mimi," Mazie pleaded, squeezing the old woman's frigid hand. "You can't go yet. It's not time. Not yet!"

"Jesus." Mimi breathed the word with a soft exhale, and the hand Mazie held in hers went limp. There was no doubt her beloved Mimi was gone. Nearly collapsing onto the side of the bed, she gathered the now lifeless body into her arms and wept.

The funeral was on Friday—a nearly packed house at the church Mimi had attended since coming to live with Lilly and Mazie a few years earlier. Edward sat on Mazie's left, her mother on her right. Each held one of her hands as the service progressed, with Mimi's favorite songs being sung and a slideshow of Mimi's life playing across the screen. Mazie knew the pastor delivered a moving eulogy, but for the life of her she couldn't concentrate or remember one word he said. She knew only that Mimi was no longer with them. She had answered the call of the angels the moment she saw Jesus, leaving the rest of them behind to miss her and long for the day when they would see her once again.

It's what she wanted. How many times did she tell me how she longed to go home, to be with Jesus and all those who had gone on before her? I know it's for the best, and I know I'll see her again someday, but ...

She blinked back tears, momentarily letting go of Edward's hand to fumble in her purse for a tissue. Where were they? She was certain she'd put some in there before leaving this morning.

Edward reached into his own pocket and pulled out a clean white handkerchief, handing it to her wordlessly. She nodded her thanks and took it, dabbing at her eyes. How long would she feel like this? Would the pain get better ... or worse? Was that even possible?

Her mind drifted back to that summer in Prattville, when she'd first met her great-grandmother and spent a long, hot summer falling in love with her. Though she knew Mimi had never really wanted to leave her home in the South, Mazie was so very glad she did. The last years they'd had together, even though Mazie had been away at school much of the time, had been so very special. She knew she would have to cling to those memories to get through the days ahead.

The service was ending now, and people were coming up to the front, passing by the closed coffin, decorated with flowers and pictures of Mimi, to bid her farewell before turning to offer their condolences to the family. Mazie did her best to hold herself together, knowing her mother was no doubt struggling to do the same. Through it all she was so thankful for Edward's strong presence beside her. And yet ... Mimi had died before telling them the end of Harriet Tubman's story. Somehow Mazie had hoped that by the time Mimi was finished, Mazie would have found the answer she was looking for, even though she still hadn't identified the question.

With her mind and heart elsewhere, Mazie dutifully turned her attention to those who stopped to speak to her or offer a hug. She wanted desperately to get through this time and get back home where she could throw herself on her bed and cry, but she knew she still had to face the graveside service at the cemetery. At the thought, she grasped Edward's hand and held on as tightly as she could.

At last, everyone had gone home—even Edward. The refrigerator was full of casseroles and salads, and the kitchen counter was lined with desserts of every description. Mazie had no appetite for any of them, though it seemed half of Langsdale had dropped by during the afternoon to help them eat it.

"You look exhausted," Lilly said, laying a hand on Mazie's shoulder.

Mazie looked into her mother's eyes, ringed with dark circles. "So do you." She glanced around the kitchen. "I don't see anything in here that needs attention before morning. Edward got everything cleaned up and put away as best he could before he left. Let's go to bed."

Lilly nodded. "Will you be all right? Can you sleep?"

She shrugged. "I don't know. Eventually, I suppose. Since Mimi died, I ..." Her voice cracked and paused before continuing. "I go to bed, thinking I'll fall asleep the minute my head hits the pillow, but then ... I end up lying there, staring at the ceiling, wondering what would have happened if I'd gone to her a few minutes sooner, or—"

"Don't," Lilly said, pulling her daughter into an embrace. "Don't even think about blaming yourself in any way. Mimi was ready, sweetheart. She wanted to go, you know that. The doctor told us her heart was failing and could stop at any time. And with all the other health issues she had going on besides, we're just blessed we had her with us as long as we did."

Mazie nodded, glad for her mother's closeness. The feeling took her back to her childhood, through every scraped knee and lost kitten, when she had no father or extended family to turn to. Always it was her mom who was there for her, working hard to provide for them and devoting her off hours to Mazie in every way she could.

Burying her face in her mother's shoulder, she let the tears come, wishing she could be stronger instead of adding to Lilly's weariness and pain. As soon as she was able, she took a few deep breaths and stepped back, swiping at her wet face with the back of her hand.

"Sorry, Mom. I meant to wait until I got to bed for that. I didn't mean to add to your burden."

Lilly smiled, her own pain overshadowed by what Mazie knew was her love and dedication to her only child. "I'm your mother. You could never be a burden to me."

She reached up and brushed back the curls from Mazie's forehead. "Come on. I'll walk you to bed, and then we can both cry ourselves to sleep."

Mazie nodded. No doubt that was exactly what would happen, but it helped to lean on her mother as they headed down the hallway.

CHAPTER TWENTY-SIX

Edward sat on his couch, staring into the darkness and praying for Mazie. He had always known she would take her great-grandmother's death hard, but now it had happened, he wanted to help her through it, yet felt helpless to do so. Though she responded well to his encouraging words or sensitive gestures, he knew she still had her wall up. If anything, she may have added an extra line of bricks to it in the past few days.

And there was more. Edward wrestled with what he knew was unreasonable disappointment over God's not letting Mimi stay long enough to finish the story about Harriet Tubman. The former matriarch of Mazie's family had indicated the night before she died there was yet more about the amazing woman named Moses, and Edward had been certain they would learn about it in the next couple of days. Now Mimi was gone. If they were to know the rest of the story, someone had to make the effort to look it up. He, no doubt, was that someone.

With a sigh, he pulled himself from the couch and padded barefoot across the room to his desk. He flipped on the light before sitting down and jostling the mouse to bring his screen to life. He immediately went to the internet and typed in Harriet Tubman's name. He was stunned at the myriad of choices her name produced. Clicking on what he imagined would be one of the most reliable sources, he soon found himself immersed in the life story of the second Moses.

Not only did his reading confirm much of what Mimi had told them, but it also filled in some of the blanks, as well as explaining how many conflicting opinions existed regarding some parts of the woman's life. But it was the part after her service in the Union Army that drew him now. He must learn the end of Harriet's story, and then pray for the right time to share it with Mazie.

One of the first things he learned was that after the war, following a volatile argument with a white man, John Tubman was shot to death, a fact that eventually reached Harriet and saddened her. She had little time to dwell on it, however, as she was busily involved in establishing a home for indigent Blacks, particularly the elderly who had no means of support. Though she applied to the government for a military pension, she was turned down and had to rely on the gifts and support of prominent individuals who admired her and the work she'd done through the years. One of them, Sarah Bradford, donated her time to write *Scenes in the Life of Harriet Tubman*. The book was self-published, financed by other friends of Harriet, including William Seward. The book was a success and produced an income that not only covered Harriet's living expenses, but also helped fund her work. Still, Harriet struggled financially until the end of her life simply because she was always ready to give away anything she had to help someone else.

Then, as Edward continued to read, he gasped at the words that seemed to jump off the page, saying Harriet had at last remarried. On March 18, 1869, Harriet became the wife of Nelson Davis, a veteran of Company G, Colored Infantry Volunteers. Though he was more than twenty years younger than Harriet, it is believed they met while she served on the South Carolina coast, and she may have cared for Nelson when he was injured or sick. In any case, he developed a great admiration for Harriet and seemed not to care about the age difference. What little is known about Nelson shows him as a kind and caring man, who helped Harriet by farming the small piece of land where her home stood.

Soon after her marriage, Harriet threw her time and energy into another cause—women's suffrage, just as Mimi had mentioned. Even as Harriet continued to fight for the rights of Blacks, she also lobbied for the right for women to vote. She sometimes shared a platform with Susan B. Anthony and Elizabeth Cady Stanton, working closely with them to give the women of America a voice.

Harriet's life seemed to be taking a turn for the better until her husband died at the young age of forty-four, once again leaving Harriet alone to continue the work the Lord had given her. Harriet's parents lived to be nearly one hundred, so one of her primary tasks was caring for them, as well as many others who showed up on her doorstep through the years. Thanks to her marriage to Nelson Davis, a Civil War veteran, she was eventually able to apply for and receive an eighty-dollar-a-month widow's pension to complement her meager income.

Harriet's fame and influence extended even beyond the borders of the United States. In 1897, she received the Diamond Jubilee medal from Queen Victoria, in honor of the queen's sixtieth anniversary on the throne. The uneducated, penniless slave girl had indeed come a long way from her master's plantation.

Edward sat back in his chair, rubbing his eyes. He knew he was nearing the end of Harriet's life story, and he wasn't sure he was quite ready to read it. At last, he decided he should, simply because he wanted the entire thing tucked away in his memory for when he felt the time was right to present it to Mazie. And so he read on.

By 1911, Harriet had become so frail she was admitted to the rest home named in her honor. "I am nearing the end of my journey," Harriet declared when she spoke to the congregation during her last visit to church. "I can hear them bells a-ringing, I can hear the angels singing, I can see the hosts a-marching, I hear someone say, 'There is one crown left and that is for Old Aunt Harriet and she shall not lose her reward.'"

After a severe bout with pneumonia, on March 10, 1913, at the age of ninety-three, Harriet closed her eyes for the last time and no doubt heard her Lord say, "Well done, good and faithful servant. Welcome home at last."

Slightly over a year later, the city of Auburn honored their beloved Harriet with a proclamation issued by the mayor to fly the flag all over the city as a tribute to the monumental work accomplished by this humble but courageous and faith-filled woman. The next day, flags flew everywhere across a city populated mostly by Whites. At Auburn's auditorium, flags were lowered to half-mast at the unveiling of a bronze tablet in Harriet's honor.

Booker T. Washington was among the attendees that day, and he said Harriet had "brought the two races nearer together, made it possible for the white race to place a higher estimate upon the black race."

By the time Edward had finished reading, tears trickled down his face. "You knew that when God made a promise, He meant it," he whispered. "Of all I learned about you, Harriet Tubman, that's the greatest thing."

It wasn't until he flipped off the light and stood up to head for bed that he realized Harriet had died at the age of ninety-three—the same age as Mimi.

"Looks like it's going to be a hot weekend," Tracy observed, as she sat out on the porch swing with Edward while they both nursed a second cup of coffee. Their parents had once again gone away for the weekend to visit relatives, and Edward had dropped by soon after sunup to keep Tracy company. She enjoyed these rare brother-sister times together and was determined to make the best of them.

Edward nodded. "Unusually so," he said. "But you know we always get a handful of days like that each summer. Most of the time the weather around here is as perfect as it gets." He smiled as a memory tugged at his heart. "Well, Mimi didn't think so. She claimed to be cold all the time since she left Alabama."

Tracy laughed. "From my one trip to the South during the summer, I'd say they can have that kind of heat. Give me the good old San Francisco fog anytime! Besides, we're far enough from the bay to get the best of both worlds—lots more sunshine than Frisco, but cool sea breezes to keep things comfy. I love it."

"Don't get me wrong," Edward said. "So do I. It was just Mimi who felt otherwise. When we'd take her out for a walk, or even in the car, she bundled up like we were heading for Alaska."

Tracy set her cup down and turned in the swing toward her big brother. "You miss her, don't you?"

He kept his face straight ahead, but she saw his jaw twitch. "More than I thought I would," he said, his hands clasped around his large coffee mug. "And it's more than just hearing her stories. I loved that and was disappointed she didn't live long enough to share the ending with us." He angled his face toward hers, his eyes glassy in the morning light. "She was a really fine lady, you know."

Tracy nodded. "From what little time I spent with her, I could tell that." She took a deep breath. "So how's Mazie taking it? Pretty hard, I imagine."

"Definitely. They were close."

"Even though they didn't spend much time together before she came to live with them a few years ago? I mean, if I remember right, didn't they spend one summer together, years ago, back in Alabama when Mazie was a child?"

"Yep, that's it. But somehow they really connected."

"You going over there later on?"

"Sure." Edward took a swig of coffee. "Now that the funeral is over and all that's left is a mess of casseroles and desserts, I think it's really going to hit her."

Tracy hesitated before asking her question. She knew Edward had definite uncrossable boundaries when it came to his relationship with Mazie. "Do you ... think she'll let you be there for her? I know you've said she tends to hold back sometimes."

A flash of pain darted through Edward's dark eyes. "I hope so." He shrugged. "I'm going to try. That's all I can do, right?"

"Right. And pray, of course."

"I do that all the time, especially when it comes to Mazie."

Tracy waited again. "So ... no progress in getting her to accept your proposal?"

"None. Sometimes, I think she seems to be moving closer, but then something happens or I say something or ... I don't know. I'm not even sure what sets her off, but the next thing I know the divide is back. I do know I can't find a way across it on my own, and believe me, I've tried. So, I just keep praying God will do something to close the gap."

She laid her hand on Edward's. "I'm praying the same thing. I like Mazie. You know that, right? But unless God intervenes and brings healing to whatever the problem is, it will never work."

Edward's shoulders drooped. "I know," he said, his eyes searching hers. "And that's the hardest part of all this. What if the healing never comes?"

She squeezed his hand, unable to offer him an answer without sounding trite. But the bottom line was either God would bring the healing needed for Edward and Mazie to get together at last ... or He would lead each of them to something or someone else.

Though Mazie had drenched her pillow with tears the night before, it had taken hours for her to fall asleep. When she awoke to the early morning light and peered at her bedside clock, her first thought was that she'd overslept. It was nearly seven thirty, and her mom needed to get to work. That meant Mazie had to get breakfast going for Mimi.

And then the memories flooded her, a reality she wished she could block out but knew she couldn't. She didn't have to get up and make breakfast for Mimi—not today, not tomorrow, not ever again. Her beloved great-grandmother was now in the presence of her Savior, and though Mazie knew she should rejoice in that fact, the only thing she felt now was a heavy, deep sense of loss.

"Oh, Mimi," she whispered, "I knew I'd miss you, but I had no idea it would be like this."

Tears nipped at her eyes again, and she rubbed them away, determined not to start on another crying jag. Since there was no reason to get up early now, perhaps she could lie here and drift back off to sleep, though she doubted it.

And then she was on a plane, wondering where she was going. She glanced around at the passengers but recognized no one. Why was she traveling alone?

She glanced down at herself and gasped. Small hands, resting in a lap that scarcely filled the seat. Was she a child again? Somehow the thought encouraged her, as she imagined her great-grandmother picking her up at the Selma airport when the plane landed.

Mimi, she thought. *Will you be there, waiting for me? Will we spend the summer together again, the way we did so many years ago?*

And then she was there, stepping out of the plane into the blinding southern sunlight, where steam rose from the tarmac and the air was heavy and sweet. She was back in Prattville, back where she'd first come to know the woman after whom she was named. And the entire long, lazy summer stretched out ahead of them, ready to be explored and enjoyed.

Mazie threw her arms into the air, despite the oppressive heat, and twirled around with delight, not at all surprised to find herself on the front porch where she'd slept as a child during her one visit to Alabama. The little makeshift bed was there, waiting for her, and Mimi sat in the rocker next to it, holding the Moses quilt in her lap. Her smile was warm and welcoming, and Mazie felt as if she'd come home for the first time in her life, though she was confused by the feeling.

"Why am I here, Mimi?" she asked, moving toward her.

"I invited you," she said, her voice clear, yet somehow far away. "I wanted you to see and to understand ... at last."

Mazie frowned. "See what? What is it I need to see and understand?"

"Just come, and then you'll know."

As Mimi spoke, she began to fade from Mazie's sight. The girl's heart raced. She couldn't lose Mimi again! Ordering her rebellious legs to move, she struggled to move toward her great-grandmother before she was gone, but she quickly found herself wrapped in some sort of blanket, making movement impossible. She stopped fighting and looked down at the covering that held her. It was the Moses quilt, spread out in front of her yet encircling her at the same time. A patch showing a dove with a branch in its beak caught her eye. What did it mean? Why hadn't Mimi told them the part of the story that explained that patch?

"Mimi," she called. "Mimi, come back! You have to tell me about the dove! Mimi, what does it mean? Mimi! Mimi, come back, please!"

She was weeping by then, as she sensed the quilt falling away, being replaced by arms that held and rocked her and a familiar voice that soothed her.

"Shh, Mazie, it's okay. I'm here, sweetheart. Mimi's gone, and she can't come back, but I'm here with you. It's okay, baby."

"Mama," Mazie sobbed, reverting to the name for her mother she hadn't used in more than a decade. "Mama, I had a dream."

"I know, sweetheart," Lilly crooned, stroking Mazie's hair. "I know you did. But you're awake now, and everything's going to be all right. Shh."

But as grateful as Mazie was for her mother's comforting embrace, she wasn't so sure everything was going to be all right—not right away—and possibly not ever. The thought stabbed her heart with fire, and she buried her face in her mother's shoulder and continued to cry.

CHAPTER TWENTY-SEVEN

By the time Edward came by to pick up Mazie for a late lunch, she had begun to formulate a plan. Did she dare voice it to anyone? Would Edward, of all people, understand what she was proposing, even when she herself didn't fully understand why she was pursuing it?

She watched him from the corner of her eye, as he kept his eyes on the road and drove toward their destination. The top was down on his convertible, a warm breeze gently lifting Mazie's hair from her neck and shoulders as they wended their way through the warm afternoon toward Fisherman's Wharf. Edward had insisted on taking her somewhere special, and she smiled at his thoughtfulness to take into consideration her passion for fresh seafood. Where could they possibly get fresher fish than at one of the many restaurants on or near the pier? Now if she could just swallow her grief long enough to eat, she might not feel like she was wasting Edward's money.

"So," he said, darting a quick glance at her, "what are you hungry for? You know they have everything imaginable there. We could do hot dogs and pretzels, or ice cream and candy ..." His voice trailed off and he grinned, turning his eyes back to the road. "Or, of course, we could try one of those nice sit-down places with tablecloths and menus."

"And shrimp," she said, surprising herself at how good that sounded.

Edward laughed. "Well, I guess I have my answer. Tablecloths, menus, and shrimp it is. I know just the place ... though there will probably be a line."

"That's okay," she said. "I don't mind waiting."

"We have the perfect weather for it. Looks like the sun is shining even on the bay—and you know how rare that is."

Mazie tried to laugh, but her effort failed. A smile was the best she could offer, and she knew he couldn't see that. So she reached over and rubbed his shoulder.

"You doing okay?" he asked, the levity gone from his voice, and she smiled at his genuine concern for her.

"As okay as can be expected." She sighed. "I ... had a dream last night. This morning, actually."

"Really? About what?"

"Mimi."

His jaw twitched.

"I was in a plane, flying somewhere, but I was just a little girl. That's when I knew I was flying to Alabama to visit Mimi. When I got off the plane, I felt the Southern heat, and I was so excited."

Edward nodded but didn't speak.

"Then I was at Mimi's house on the porch where I slept on those hot nights. Mimi was there, sitting in the rocker beside my bed, holding the Moses quilt on her lap. She ... told me I needed to come ... so I could understand. I asked her what I needed to understand, but then I was wrapped in the quilt."

She shook her head. "I couldn't figure out what the dream meant then, but now it makes sense."

Mazie paused, trying to work up the courage to say what would no doubt sound bizarre to Edward's ears. At last she opened her mouth and did her best to voice her thoughts. "I believe I'm supposed to go to Alabama. To Gee's Bend—Boykin, specifically—where the quilts are made. Where Mimi bought the Moses quilt."

Watching Edward's profile, she saw his eyebrow rise. She waited.

"I think you're right," he said at last. "I think you should go to Gee's Bend. And I think I should go with you. It's what Mimi would want. And in some strange way, I think it's what Harriet would want too."

Mazie's head was reeling. So much had happened so quickly. She scarcely remembered the seafood meal she and Edward had shared the previous Saturday. All she could think of at the time was that he was going to Alabama with her—to Gee's Bend. Would the trip clarify the questions and provide the answers she'd apparently been seeking all these years, even though the search had only recently begun to come into focus for her?

Sitting beside Edward on the plane bound for the Selma airport, she knew he had his own concerns about the trip. No doubt a big part of those concerns had to do with her reaction to whatever they discovered while they were there. Would she at last be at peace with herself and able to commit to a life with him? Though she was not yet ready to admit it, she hoped that would be the outcome.

She thought back to that Saturday evening, just over a week ago, after they returned from their outing at Fisherman's Wharf. When they'd broken the news to Lilly, she'd seemed strangely unsurprised by it, as if she'd been expecting it all along. She asked only that they go with open hearts and minds and assured them she would be praying for them while they were gone.

Edward's sister and parents had promised the same thing, though Tracy seemed to be the most skeptical about the entire thing. "Exactly what do you expect to find there you can't find right here?" Tracy had asked. Mazie had been unable to give her an answer, except to say she knew she had to go.

We'll be landing in Selma in the drop-dead heat of summer. Just like I did so many years ago, and the way I did in my dream. Oh, Lord, please guide us into all You've purposed for us there!

Edward took her hand, and she looked up at him, surprised to realize he was awake. He'd been sitting so quietly with his eyes closed, she'd assumed he was napping. She squeezed his hand in thanks, wanting him to know yet again how very much she appreciated his support, particularly since neither of them had any assurances of the outcome of their venture.

Just come, and then you'll know, Mimi had intoned in Mazie's dream.

Know what? What do I need to know? Mazie had asked herself that question more times than she could count, but she had yet to come up with an answer of any kind. Was she about to find it at last? And if she did, would she regret having pursued it?

She sighed and leaned back against the headrest. They still had more than an hour until they landed. She might as well try to catch a little sleep in the interim.

Unlike her dream, Mazie didn't step off the plane onto the steaming tarmac, slapped in the face by hot, humid, heavy air. Instead she and Edward walked in air-conditioned comfort through the skyway into the airport, where they followed the signs to baggage claim and from there toward the door marked Ground Transportation to find their rental car.

As they stepped into the space immediately in front of the automatic doors, a whoosh flung the doors open and catapulted them into the sweltering soup Southerners called air. Mazie caught her breath, realizing how much worse it was than she had remembered. She glanced up at Edward, whose eyes were wide and whose forehead was already starting to pop with beads of sweat.

"Over there," he said, gesturing toward the sign that identified their car rental company. Pulling their suitcases behind them, they pressed toward their goal. Mazie wondered how Mimi—or anyone, for that matter—could miss this type of weather, regardless of how long she lived here.

At last they stepped inside a small office, where a window air conditioner whirred at full speed. With only one other person in line ahead of them, it didn't take long to sign the papers and obtain their keys. One more short trip outside into the heat and they'd be on their way in the cool comfort of a rented sedan.

With the suitcases loaded into the trunk and the car's AC blasting, Edward backed out of the space and headed for the airport exit while Mazie punched their destination into the built-in GPS. With no accommodation available in the tiny community of Gee's Bend, Mazie and Edward had reserved two rooms at a motel about thirty miles from their destination. They'd check in, find somewhere to have dinner, and get some sleep before driving to the little hamlet where Mazie prayed they would find someone who could help them in their vague quest for answers.

She glanced at Edward, once again sitting behind the wheel of a car and taking her where she wanted to go. During their flight, he had filled her in on what he'd learned about the remainder of Harriet Tubman's remarkable life. It had helped to hear the end of the woman's story, but she realized that even if Mimi had lived long enough to tell it to her, it wouldn't have been enough to quell her unease. What happened on this trip might be her last chance to find the peace she so desperately desired.

Please, Lord, guide us to the right people and places. Show me—show us*—what you want us to see, Father.*

A strange sensation of dancing butterflies and warm honey swirled in her stomach, nearly overwhelming her with anticipation. Was it God Himself, reassuring her He had heard her prayer and would answer? As they continued on their way, she willed it to be so.

CHAPTER TWENTY-EIGHT

Tuesday morning dawned hot and heavy. Mazie was convinced the sweet smell of the magnolia bushes in front of their motel had somehow permeated the heavy door and closed windows of her room. Telling herself that was impossible didn't help. When she was in the South, she smelled magnolias. Period.

She pulled herself from bed, anxious to get started on their day. Edward had told her to call him when she was up and almost ready to go, since he could get ready a lot faster than she. They'd grab a quick breakfast before they left, and then drive on out to Gee's Bend—Boykin, as the little hamlet was named—and see if they could find anyone who knew anything about the Moses quilt and the lady or ladies who worked on it.

She showered and dressed and gave Edward a ring. He answered right away, assuring her he was ready to go when she was. Within minutes, they were sitting at the twenty-four-hour café next to the motel—Edward working hard to convince her she really would like grits if she'd just give them a try. She chose fresh fruit instead and left the grits to him.

"You're in the South, Mazie," he teased after they placed their order. "Southerners eat grits, not fresh fruit."

She wrinkled her nose. "Well, I'm not a Southerner, and I don't eat grits. Fruit is good for you."

He grinned. "Suit yourself. I'm in the South, and I'm going to take full advantage of it."

"I noticed. You didn't just order grits but biscuits and gravy too. You're not going to fit in your clothes by the time we go home."

"You could be right," he countered, "but I'll bet I have more fun with my meals than you do."

She ignored him, sipping her coffee while they waited for their food. She was too nervous to eat and wondered if she'd even be able to get the fruit down. The thought of what they might—or might not—find when they got to Gee's Bend had been buzzing through her mind all morning. It's a wonder she'd gotten any sleep at all the night before.

By the time their food arrived, Edward proclaimed himself hungry enough to eat a horse, and he gave every impression of trying to do so, wolfing down his grits and biscuits and gravy with gusto. Mazie picked at her fruit and nibbled on her toast, anxious to get on with the day, yet nearly terrified to do so.

They were back on the road by nine o'clock, motoring along at a steady pace and marveling at the lush scenery. When Edward announced they had arrived on the outskirts of Boykin, Mazie's stomach clenched. Now what? They'd come this far—she couldn't turn back now. But where did they start? Whom should they approach? What would they say? More important, when the day came to an end, would she be any closer to unraveling and answering the questions that plagued her than when they'd first stepped aboard the plane in San Francisco?

There was only one way to find out, she told herself, taking a deep breath as Edward pulled the car to a stop in front of what appeared to be an old general store. She was about to reach for the door handle when Edward grabbed her other hand and squeezed.

"It's going to be okay, baby," he said.

She nodded and turned back to open the door, ready to get on with it.

Not a breath of breeze stirred the thick, steamy air as Edward and Mazie left their car and stepped into the humble store, a bell attached to the door tinkling an announcement of their arrival. Mazie squinted until her eyes adjusted to the inside light, more muted than the glaring sunshine outside and, thankfully, much cooler as well.

She'd nearly given up waiting when a short man, his skin more gray than black, bent by years and wrinkled beyond counting, stepped through the curtains from another room. Nodding a greeting as he approached them, Mazie couldn't help but notice how few teeth lined his otherwise warm smile.

"Welcome," he said, his faded eyes darting from Edward to Mazie and back again. "What can I do for y'all?"

Mazie opened her mouth but found speaking impossible. When Edward jumped in, she breathed a silent thanks.

"My name is Edward Clayton," he said, reaching out his hand for a shake, which was heartily received by their host. "This is my girlfriend, Mazie Hartford." He paused as the old man shook Mazie's hand and introduced himself as Moe and welcomed them to Gee's Bend. When Moe said no more, Edward continued. "We're here on a sort of personal agenda. Mazie has just lost her great-grandmother, who was from these parts. Well, Prattville. But before she died, she showed us a quilt she had purchased from someone here in Gee's Bend. She called it the Moses quilt. It told the life of Harriet Tubman. Now Mimi—Mazie's great-grandmother—has passed on and left the quilt behind. We wanted to see if we could connect with the person who made the quilt—or at least the one who sold it to her. Is that possible? Would you have any idea how we might go about such a thing?"

Mazie had watched Moe perk up at the mention of Harriet Tubman, and her heart rate elevated accordingly. Had they stumbled on the right place and met the right person on their very first try? It seemed impossible, but in such a small town perhaps it wasn't unlikely at all.

"I remember that quilt," Moe said, his eyes showing signs of life. "Sure 'nough. Most of the Gee's Bend quilts are about local history, but the Moses quilt was different." He smiled and nodded, and Mazie thought he looked as if he was remembering something. "Several of the ladies worked on sewing the bottom of that quilt together, but Miss Bessie was who pieced the top. She was a strong admirer of old Moses."

"Was?" The word popped from Mazie's mouth before she could stop it. "You mean ... Miss Bessie's ... dead?"

Moe laughed. "Why, no, ma'am, she's not dead at all, though most thought she would be by now. She's got to be nearing a hundred but won't tell anyone exactly how close she is." He paused. "I can give y'all her address if you'd like."

"That would be great," Edward said. "And a phone number too, please. We should call before we drop in, don't you think?"

Moe laughed again. "Miss Bessie don't have no phone. Don't believe in 'em. Says if anyone wants to talk to her, they can just come on over."

Edward and Mazie exchanged eyebrow-arched glances while Moe wrote the address on a piece of paper.

"Do you think she'll be home?" Edward asked, glancing at the address before pocketing it.

Moe grinned. "I know she is. She don't hardly go nowhere 'cept church on Sunday. Several of the ladies in town take her meals and check on her every day, but otherwise she just stays home."

"Alone?" Mazie asked.

"Sure thing," Moe said. "Though her five dogs keep her company."

Edward cleared his throat. "Do you think the dogs will be a problem? I mean, since we can't call ahead, will it be all right to just walk up to her house and knock on the door?"

"Don't know how else you'd get in," Moe said. "That's what I do when I drop by for a visit. Ain't been bit by one of those dogs yet."

Mazie wasn't comforted by his words, and something told her Edward wasn't either.

"Can you ... point us in the right direction?" Edward asked.

"Sure thing." Moe came out from behind the counter and headed for the door. "Come on. I'll show you."

Within minutes, Edward and Mazie were back in the car, following Moe's simple directions toward Miss Bessie's place—"head straight down this here road and turn left just past the peach orchard"—while Mazie wondered what in the world she'd been thinking when she decided to come on this trip.

A lone bird, most likely a hawk Mazie imagined, circled above the old house as she and Edward sat in the front seat, working up the courage to get out and brave the rickety porch, not to mention the so-far unseen five dogs.

Edward took her hand. "Shall we pray first?"

She nodded and closed her eyes. "Yes, please."

"Father God," Edward said, his voice calming the flutter in Mazie's heart, "we believe You brought us here for a reason, so we're asking You to go ahead of us as we approach the woman known as Miss Bessie. Help us to know what to say, what to ask, Lord, and please give Miss Bessie a receptive heart. Show us what You want us to learn here, Father. Use this visit for Your glory, please Lord. Amen."

Mazie opened her eyes, relieved and reassured by Edward's brief but humble prayer, though she wished he would have included a request for protection from the five dogs.

"Well," Edward said with a sigh. "I guess we'd better get on with it."

He opened the door and stepped out onto the dusty driveway, making his way around the front of the car to the passenger side. He had just reached for the door handle when an explosion of barking, growling sentries burst on the scene, heading straight for him.

Mazie's eyes opened wide, as sharp needles of fear shot up her spine. Would the dogs attack Edward? What could she do to help? Edward seemed frozen in place, his hand unmoving on the car's door handle.

She was about to open the door herself and order him inside, even if he had to climb in on her lap, when the off-kilter screen door squeaked open, and a tiny, dark figure on a cane appeared in the entrance.

"Beauregard! Brutus! You dogs get over here and bring the rest of that worthless pack with you. Can't you see we have company?"

Her voice was just strong enough to reach Mazie's ears, but apparently the dogs heard it loud and clear. Their barking and growling stopped immediately, followed by a few snuffles and whines as they turned from Edward and made their way toward the porch, heads bowed and tails tucked. Mazie breathed a huge sigh of relief, even as she wondered what Edward would do next.

Before she could find out, the old woman called out, "Well, what're y'all waitin' for? Come on inside. It's too hot to stand 'round out there."

Edward turned to Mazie and raised his eyebrows, but she could tell he was swallowing a smile. He opened the door, and she joined him as they approached the tiny home. The dogs lay quietly now, on and around the porch, though Mazie was certain they'd like nothing better than to be allowed to chew on their visitors for lunch. She clung to Edward's arm as they mounted the stairs.

"I knowed y'all was comin'," the old woman said. "The good Lord done tol' me so this mornin'."

Mazie smiled. So God really was in this after all.

Edward took the lead. "I'm Edward Clayton, and this is Mazie Hartford. We're from California, and Moe down at the store told us where we could find you. You must be Miss Bessie."

"Must be," she said, as she leaned on her cane and motioned them inside. "So old Moe sent y'all, eh?" She chuckled. "Most everybody stops there when they come into Gee's Bend for the first time. Good thing too, 'cause Moe knows everything and everybody in town."

She ushered them to a worn wooden table in a corner that served as a kitchen. "Sit down. I got some cold lemonade ready for y'all. Fixed it soon as the good Lord tol' me y'all was comin'."

Mazie marveled at the women's simple faith and waited with Edward at the table while Miss Bessie set out three Mason jars and a pitcher of lemonade.

"Here, let me pour that," Mazie offered, reaching for the pitcher.

Miss Bessie nodded her permission and joined them at the table.

"Now then," she said, once they each had a full glass of cold liquid in front of them, "why would two young people like yourselves come so far to see Miss Bessie? Been askin' myself that question all mornin'. Asked the good Lord too, but He didn't answer. Just said to be ready for y'all, so here I am."

"We appreciate that," Edward said. "And you're right. We've come a long way to talk to you. It's about a quilt you made. Mazie's great-grandma bought it from you some years ago. She called it the Moses quilt."

The old woman's eyes lit up, and a smile spread across her face, nearly erasing the wrinkles that crisscrossed her dark skin. She nodded slowly as she spoke. "The Moses quilt. An act of love, that was. I pieced the top myself, you know."

"Yes," Mazie said. "Moe told us that."

"'Course, several of us worked on the backing like we always do. But the top was just me. Took me a long time, but I wanted it to be jus' right—to honor a great woman."

"Mimi, Mazie's great-grandmother, used your quilt to tell us Harriet Tubman's story," Edward explained.

"She did?" Miss Bessie seemed pleased. "Well now, I do remember your great-grandma," she said, turning to

Mazie. "Been many years since she bought that quilt. Can't rightly remember how many, but I do remember she was a beautiful and gracious lady."

Mazie's eyes stung with tears. "Yes, she was," she said, choking back a sob.

Miss Bessie's smile faded and her eyes narrowed. "Has she passed on then?"

Mazie nodded. "A couple of weeks ago."

The woman's hand stretched across the table and came to rest on Mazie's. "Then she be with Jesus now."

Mazie nodded again, still unable to speak.

Miss Bessie patted her hand. "We be glad for her, but sad for us. I know 'bout sad. Lost most of my loved ones over the years, even my children. I be 'bout the only one left in my family now. So hard, baby." She patted her hand again, and Mazie's heart warmed as she realized the woman's sincerity born out of her own grief.

Edward jumped in then as he took another sip of lemonade and set the glass down in front of him. "Miss Bessie, Mazie and I were wondering ... I mean, is there anything about the quilt Mimi might not have told us? She ... passed on before she finished telling us the whole story. Now we feel like something's missing, as if the quilt holds some key that will unlock a secret in Mazie's past." He paused. "Something she really needs to know."

Miss Bessie raised her almost nonexistent eyebrows as she looked from one to the other before answering. "You two plannin' to get married?" she asked.

Mazie caught her breath. Where had that come from?

Edward recovered first. "Well, I ..." He cleared his throat. "We're talking about it."

Miss Bessie nodded. "I thought so." She smiled. "I believe I know what your Mimi wanted you to learn. And it really ain't 'bout the quilt at all. It's 'bout what she told me when she bought it." She leaned forward, as if she were about to reveal some sort of sacred confidence. Mazie and Edward leaned forward in response.

"It's your family," Miss Bessie said, looking straight at Mazie. "Your ancestors and the reason your Mimi wanted that quilt."

Mazie held her breath, her heart tattooing against her ribcage. Was she truly about to learn the family secret she'd expected existed but no one seemed able to confirm or reveal? And once she knew it ... what then? She swallowed and waited.

"There was a connection between your family and Harriet Tubman," Miss Bessie said, and then paused before continuing.

"You mean ..." Mazie began, "we were related in some way?" The thought her ancestors might have been slaves at some point—Black and not White—had teased her imagination for years, but she'd never acknowledged it until now. It would explain the secrecy, she thought, not to mention her dark, almost kinky hair and dark eyes. Was that what Mimi had planned to tell her if she hadn't died first? If so, how would Edward take the news when he realized they had a lot more in common than either of them had realized?

Miss Bessie shook her head. "Oh, no, baby, not that. Your ancestors weren't related to Harriet or any of the other slaves. They were related to one of Harriet's masters."

Mazie gasped, her eyes going wide as the room seemed to spin around her. She was descended from slave owners, from the very ones who tortured and tormented Harriet Tubman and countless others? No, it couldn't be!

Slowly, she turned her head toward Edward. His dark eyes were already focused on her, unbelief and pain mingling there as the two of them sat at Miss Bessie's old kitchen table, speechless. They had indeed discovered the secret they'd come looking for, and Mazie realized at that moment certain things in her life would never be the same again.

CHAPTER 29

Lilly arrived home from work Wednesday evening to find Edward's car sitting in the driveway. She smiled, despite her tired feet and growling stomach. It had been a very long day, during which a granola bar served as lunch, but now her daughter was back safe and sound, and that was all that mattered.

"Welcome home," she called as she opened the front door and stepped inside. She stopped short, coming face-to-face with Edward in the entryway.

"You're back," she said, smiling as she reached out to embrace him. "I can't wait to hear all about it."

Edward's smile seemed stiff, and Lilly felt the first pangs of concern. "I'll let Mazie fill you in," he said. "I just came by to drop her off, and now, I need to get home and unpack, so I can go in to work early tomorrow." He bent to kiss her cheek before leaving. "Talk to you later," he said, and he was gone.

Lilly stood still for a moment, questions swirling through her mind before she determined to dismiss them and give Mazie a chance to tell her about their trip. "Mazie?" she called. "Where are you?"

Her daughter's voice drifted down the hallway from her room. "I'm in here putting my suitcase away. Be right there, Mom."

Good. Mazie's voice sounded normal. Maybe everything was all right after all.

Lilly went into the kitchen and opened the refrigerator. She was glad she'd thought to fix a casserole the night before. She could toss the leftovers in the microwave, and she and Mazie could be eating in minutes.

She was setting plates on the table and waiting for the microwave's ding when Mazie entered the room.

"Hey, Mom," she said, coming up behind her. "I'm so glad to see you."

Lilly turned and pulled her child into a hug. "So am I. I know you were only gone for a few days, but it seemed like so much longer. This house was empty without ..." She paused, blinking away the threat of tears. "Without you here."

Mazie's face reflected her understanding. "And Mimi too. I know what you mean."

Lilly smiled, determined to stay cheerful. "So, tell me you haven't eaten yet. I've got leftover casserole in the microwave. It's just about ready."

"It smells great. And no, I haven't eaten. We came straight here from the airport."

"Wonderful. Then we can sit down here together and talk about your trip while we eat."

The timer on the microwave sounded, so Mazie grabbed potholders and carried the casserole dish to the table while Lilly poured a couple glasses of iced tea. They sat down, offered a brief prayer of thanks, and dug in.

"This is delicious, Mom," Mazie said. "You know chicken-cheese casserole is my favorite."

"I do." Lilly smiled. "I made it especially for you—though I thought Edward might stay to have some with us."

A flicker of pain passed through Mazie's eyes, and the misgivings in Lilly's heart returned. Something was wrong between them. Had something happened on their trip? Had they had a fight or disagreement of some sort? Lilly knew the two of them seldom quarreled and seemed to get along so well, so it must have been serious to cause a rift between them. She bit back the comments and questions that longed to surface, waiting instead for Mazie to offer an explanation.

"He ... needed to get home and get ready for work tomorrow," Mazie said, poking at her food with her fork. "It's been a long day, and we were both tired."

Lilly nodded. Apparently, that was all the explanation she was going to get at this point, and she would have to honor that. "So tell me about the trip," she said, forcing a smile into her voice. "I want to hear all about Gee's Bend and its famous quilts, especially the Moses quilt."

Mazie's smile seemed stiff, but Lilly tried to overlook it. She listened to her daughter recount their meeting with a man named Moe, who directed them to Miss Bessie, an almost ageless woman, according to Mazie's description. Amazingly, Miss Bessie had been involved in the making of the Moses quilt and had met Mimi when she bought it.

Mazie's voice drifted off then, and Lilly waited. Finally she said, "Sweetheart, is something wrong?"

Her daughter's eyes misted over, and Lilly knew she was struggling for control. At last she said, "Mom, there's more. Something about our family—our ancestors." A tear slipped from her eye to her cheek, and Lilly resisted the urge to wipe it away with her finger. Instead she took a deep breath and listened as Mazie told her about ancestors neither of them had ever known existed—ancestors whose lives and beliefs challenged everything the two women believed or practiced. When Mazie had finished, Lilly suddenly understood the issue that had come between her daughter and Edward, and she prayed their love would be strong enough to overcome it.

Edward groaned when he opened his front door and found Tracy standing there. Why had he bothered to answer the bell at all? He hadn't been home for fifteen minutes, and now his little sister was there, no doubt wanting to hear all about the trip. Well, he was in no mood to talk about it.

Tracy raised her eyebrows and perched her hands on her hips. "So, you going to invite me in or make me stand out here all night?"

"Sorry," he mumbled. "I just got home a few minutes ago, and I'm kind of busy unpacking."

"Too busy for your favorite sister?" she teased, stepping past him. "Come on, now. How long have we known each other? That's not your busy face I'm seeing. Something's wrong, and I'm not leaving till I know what it is."

She folded her arms across her chest and stood in front of him, waiting.

He sighed and shook his head. "Really, Sis, I'm just tired. It's been a long day. We had to change planes twice, and—"

"Save it for somebody who believes you," she said, interrupting him mid thought. "Now come and sit down and tell me what's really going on."

Their eyes locked. "Fine," he said at last. "Let's go sit in the kitchen. I could use a cup of coffee."

"Have you eaten?" Tracy asked, leading the way. "I'll put the coffee on and fix you a sandwich if you haven't."

"No, I haven't eaten," he admitted, "but I'm really not hungry."

"Oh, please," she said. "Not hungry? That'll be the day. Now sit down and tell me what happened while I get the coffee and grub going."

Knowing there was no use trying to dissuade her, Edward plunked down at the table. Part of him wanted to tell Tracy exactly what had happened—what Miss Bessie had told them about Mazie's ancestors and how that news had driven a wedge between him and Mazie that seemed to be more than Edward was willing to fight. The other part of him wanted to run to his bedroom, lock the door, and stay there until his nosy sister finally gave up and left. The problem with that was he knew Tracy would outlast him. Might as well get it over with.

As the coffee dripped into the pot, and Tracy spread mustard and mayo on bread, Edward gave her a brief rundown of the trip, ending with Miss Bessie's revelation about Mazie's family history. The look of shock on Tracy's face seemed to validate his own reaction.

"So what are you going to do about it?" Tracy asked when he finished, coming to join him at the table.

"What do you mean?"

Tracy shrugged. "I mean, you two went back there to try to get things resolved for Mazie in hopes you could finally move on with your lives, including marriage. Now I'm getting the impression it's not so much Mazie who needs to resolve some things but you." She leaned close. "So, are you going to deal with it? Or are you going to let it come between you permanently?"

The words started a buzzing in Edward's ears, but he could think of nothing to say in reply. Instead he picked up the sandwich Tracy had placed before him and bit off enough that he couldn't possibly talk for a minute or two. He needed time to think before he said another word.

Mazie sat in the kitchen, freshly showered and sipping coffee while she wondered what to do with herself all day, let alone for the next few weeks now she didn't have Mimi to care for. Her mother had already gone to work, and it would be nearly a month before Mazie started her new teaching job. The coming days stretched out long and lonely in her mind. Worst of all, she was certain she'd lost Edward. Nothing had been the same between them since Miss Bessie told them about Mazie's ancestors. And who could blame Edward for taking it so hard? He had waited so patiently for her all this time, while she struggled to identify the questions in her heart that held her back from fully committing herself to their relationship. Now the truth had been unraveled at last, and it seemed the answers she'd been seeking were the very ones that would destroy any future she and Edward might have together.

The doorbell snagged her attention, and she frowned, glancing at her watch. Eight-thirty in the morning. Who in the world might that be?

She could hear Mimi's voice, telling her to stop sitting there wondering and go answer the door and find out. Pushing away the memories and the flood of emotions that accompanied every reminder of her absent great-grandmother, Mazie headed for the front door and pulled it open.

"Hey," Edward said, looking nearly as lost and forlorn as Mazie felt.

"Hey, yourself," she answered. "What are you doing here? I thought you'd be at work by now."

"I should be, but I thought coming here was more important."

A flicker of hope caught fire in her heart, and she pushed the screen open, beckoning him inside. He'd no sooner entered and stood in front of her than her flicker of hope turned to a stab of alarm. Had he come to formally end their relationship? She couldn't blame him if he had, particularly after she'd stalled him for so many months. Nearly holding her breath, she raised her eyes to his.

"I've been thinking about Harriet Tubman nearly all night," he said. "About how humble and courageous she was, about how she lived what she believed, and how some people say there was no one who did more to heal relationships between Blacks and Whites than she did." Tears pooled in his eyes. "I also thought about all she sacrificed and suffered to fulfill God's calling on her life." He put his hands on Mazie's arms. "We don't even begin to know what hardships are compared to someone like her. But I do know one thing, Mazie Hartford. I love you, and I don't want to live without you. This isn't about my ancestors or yours or anyone else for that matter. This is about us. You and me, and God, who I believe brought us together. But I'm not going to wait anymore. You found out what you went to Gee's Bend to discover, so I want an answer now. Today." He swallowed, the pressure of his grip on her arms tightening slightly. "Will you marry me or not, Mazie?"

She knew the tears she saw reflected in Edward's eyes were mirrored in her own, as her heart soared into newfound freedom. They were not bound by the past. Christ had set them free, even as He had with Harriet Tubman and so many others through the centuries. And somehow, as she stood there in the entryway, gazing up at the man she loved, she could hear Harriet and Mimi proclaiming in unison, "Stop fooling around, child, and just say yes!"

Mazie couldn't stop the smile that spread across her face. "Yes," she whispered at last, surprised she could get any sound past the lump in her throat. "Yes, I will marry you. And the sooner, the better."

Edward's eyes went wide, and he pulled her against his chest. She felt the laughter coming up from deep within him, even as it rang in her ears. And though the two of them stood alone at that moment, Mazie felt as if they were surrounded by a great cloud of witnesses.

EPILOGUE

Family and friends had gathered at the church Mazie and her mother had attended for so many years—the same sanctuary where just months earlier they had held a memorial service for her beloved Mimi. With the pastor from Mazie's church as well as the one from Edward's performing the ceremony together, Mazie and Edward stood with their backs to the crowd. Behind the two pastors she could see the large wooden cross on the wall. Just underneath hung an unusual adornment, one she and Edward had requested for the ceremony.

The Moses quilt held a place of honor, reminding them of all they had learned as they'd become acquainted with the various patches on the quilt, each representing a different segment in the life of a courageous, faith-filled woman. One patch caught her eye—the one with the dove holding a branch in its beak. A symbol of peace. Somehow she knew that one was meant for them—for herself and Edward and all who had gathered there that day.

She smiled as she realized the quilt also served as a reminder to all present that God is greater than any obstacle any of them could ever face. If they lived their lives as Harriet Tubman did—believing God would indeed do exactly as He said—then anything was possible.

With Edward's hand wrapped around hers, Mazie whispered a soft thank you to the two women who had made such an impact on her life—and who had both died at the age of ninety-three. *Father, may I serve You as faithfully as Harriet and Mimi,* she prayed silently, *however many years I spend on this earth.*

THE END

ABOUT THE AUTHOR

    With women's ministry as one of her primary interests, **Kathi Macias** is a popular speaker for women's retreats, conferences, and churches. An award-winning author, Kathi has written more than 50 books, including the 2011 Golden Scrolls Novel of the Year, *Red Ink*. A wife, mother, grandmother, and great-grandmother, Kathi enjoys knitting blankets and scarves for her friends and family. She and her husband, Al, call Southern California home.

NOTES

Chapter 7

1. Sarah Bradford, Harriet Tubman: The Moses of Her People (first published 1869; reprint, Secaucus, N.J.: The Citadel Press, 1961), 25.

2. Bradford, Harriet Tubman, 24.

Chapter 10

3. Earl Conrad, Harriet Tubman (Washington, D.C.: The Associated Publishers, Inc., 1943), 9.

4. Conrad, Harriet Tubman, 9.

Chapter 11

5. Rebecca Price Janney, Harriet Tubman (Minneapolis, MN: Bethany House Publishers, 1999), 33.

Chapter 20

.6. Charles L. Blockson, The Underground Railroad (New York: Prentice Hall Press, 1987), 98.

7. Henry J. Merriman, "Farewell, Farewell," 1870-1885, Library of Congress, Music Division, Public Domain.

8. Blockson, Underground, 19.

Chapter 21

9. Rebecca Price Janney, Great Women in American History (Camp Hill, PA: Horizon Books, 1996), 228.

Chapter 22

10. Bradford, Harriet Tubman, 31–32.

11. Judith Nies, Seven Women: Portraits From the American Radical Tradition (New York: Viking Press, 1977), 43.

Chapter 23

12. Conrad, Harriet Tubman, 71.

13. Conrad, Harriet Tubman, 107.

Chapter 24

14. Eugene Genovese, et al., The World the Slaves Made (New York: Vintage Books, 1972), 438.

Chapter 26

15. Conrad, Harriet Tubman, 223.

16. Conrad, Harriet Tubman, 225.

www.ingramcontent.com/pod-product-compliance
Lightning Source LLC
Chambersburg PA
CBHW061426030726
47503CB00005B/1320